D0174839

WITHDRAWN

Also by Kelly Jones

Unusual Chickens for the Exceptional Poultry Farmer

Murder, Magic, and What We Wore

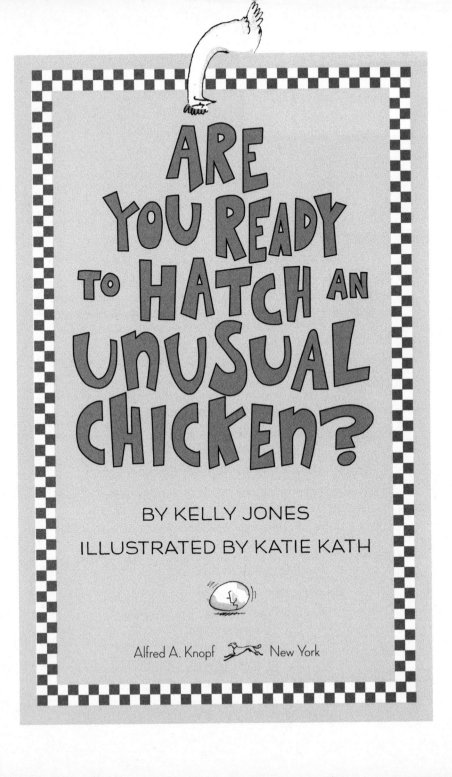

ARE YOU READY TO HATCH AN UNUSUAL CHICKEN?

BY KELLY JONES

ILLUSTRATED BY KATIE KATH

Alfred A. Knopf · New York

T 131288

VISTA GRANDE
PUBLIC LIBRARY

THIS IS A BORZOI BOOK PUBLISHED BY ALFRED A. KNOPF

This is a work of fiction. Names, characters, places, and incidents either are the product of the author's imagination or are used fictitiously. Any resemblance to actual persons, living or dead, events, or locales is entirely coincidental.

Text copyright © 2018 by Kelly Jones
Jacket art and interior illustrations copyright © 2018 by Katie Kath

All rights reserved. Published in the United States by Alfred A. Knopf, an imprint of Random House Children's Books, a division of Penguin Random House LLC, New York.

Knopf, Borzoi Books, and the colophon are registered trademarks of Penguin Random House LLC.

Visit us on the Web! rhcbooks.com

Educators and librarians, for a variety of teaching tools, visit us at RHTeachersLibrarians.com

Library of Congress Cataloging-in-Publication Data is available upon request.
ISBN 978-1-5247-6591-0 (trade) — ISBN 978-1-5247-6592-7 (lib. bdg.) — ISBN 978-1-5247-6593-4 (ebook)

The text of this book is set in 10.5-point Clarion.

Printed in the United States of America
November 2018
10 9 8 7 6 5 4 3 2 1

First Edition

Random House Children's Books
supports the First Amendment and celebrates the right to read.

For Eric, who agreed we should get chickens, and who

helped me through everything that came after.

For my parents and my brother, who believed I could do

anything. Guess you were right.

And for my cousins, my uncles, my aunts, and

my grandparents, who've always been there for me.

Thank you all so much.

INSTRUCTIONS (VERY IMPORTANT!!!):

1. Bring the unopened crate into the chickens' new run.
2. Open the crate carefully.
3. Remove the wire cage from the crate.
4. Add chicken food and water to the cage and then close it immediately, without allowing any chickens to escape.
5. Allow the chickens to observe their new home through the wire for one hour before opening the cage.
6. Let the chickens out. Observe them, and record your notes.

creeeek...

POW

Date: Friday, August 1
To: Hortensia James <hjames@APeculiarKindofBird.com>
From: Sophie Brown <unusualchickenfarmer@gmail.com>
Subject: New chickens

Dear Hortensia,

The two new chickens arrived today. I tried to follow your instructions, but as soon as I opened the cage door to add their food and water, they got out—so fast I couldn't even see them move. Or, maybe they weren't just fast. . . . What exactly are their superpowers? (I think I know, but I'd like you to tell me.)

One other problem: I only have one henhouse, so they're going to have to live with my flock. Will that be okay for now?

Thank you for sending me chickens. I hope you don't miss them too much. I'll take very good care of them.

Sincerely,
Sophie

PS What breed are they?

PPS I think I'm going to call them Aquí and Allí. (That means "Here" and "There" in Spanish, in case you didn't know.)

Date: Saturday, August 2
To: Sophie Brown <unusualchickenfarmer@gmail.com>
From: Hortensia James <hjames@APeculiarKindofBird.com>
Subject: RE: New chickens

Dear Sophie,

The hens I sent you can join your other hens but should be kept separate from roosters, since cross-breeding unusual chickens can lead to wildly unpredictable (and often dangerous) results. I'd wait until you have all the Redwood Farm chickens established before breeding new varieties. The Unusual Poultry Committee keeps a close eye on new owners of unusual poultry farms, and they prefer to have a breeding plan submitted before any new crosses are made.

Unusual poultry farmers always send chickens and eggs to their colleagues to observe and raise on their own, without commentary (aside from safety concerns). This is not a test of you or your skill. It's a scientific practice of gathering observations from many sources, rather than relying on just one written source that's passed down through many people. It helps us notice if some important observation was missed by a previous keeper, or if the breed has changed in some way. Not everyone will notice every detail, so together we create a more complete record of these amazing birds.

The breeds I'm sending you are the beginner-level unusual chicken breeds Agnes left in my care; these chickens should not require any special safety measures.

Once you have observed them for a period of time (one year is usual), you'll receive a list of contacts for other farmers who've observed that breed, so you can compare notes. Please contact me if you have health or safety concerns in the meantime.

I'm attaching my preliminary observation form as a starting point, but feel free to record your research in any format you choose, and to go above and beyond these questions.

I'll ship the first batch of your eggs ASAP. Get your incubator ready!

Sincerely,
Hortensia

PS Forgive me for asking, but you did complete your apprenticeship with Agnes, right? And earn your Unusual Poultry certification from the Committee?

Poultry breed observations by: Sophie Brown, unusual poultry farmer

Observations made: Saturday, August 2

Type of bird: My friend Chris says they look like Blue Coppers, maybe Marans?

Gender of bird: Chris says they look like hens.

PLEASE RECORD YOUR NOTES ABOUT THE FOLLOWING:

Comb: pinkish red and pointy

Beak: gray and pointy

Eyes: orange with black pupils

Wattles: red

Earlobes: red

Beard: Chris says they don't have beards. (I didn't know chickens could have beards. Especially girl chickens. But he says some breeds have puffy feather beards, even the hens.)

Head: orange

Neck: mostly orange with a little gray

Body: gray

Tail: gray, points up

Legs and Feet: gray with a few feathers (not nearly as many as Roadrunner)

comb

earlobe

beak

wattle

tail points up!

Eggs: dark brown, almost chocolate-colored shells, but regular eggs inside (Too.bad! It would be pretty great to have chocolate eggs every day.)

Typical movements: They walk around, and then suddenly they're in a different spot, only you can't see them move there.

Typical vocalizations (if any): They bawk like my other chickens. Louder than Chameleon, but quieter than Henrietta.

Interactions with other poultry:
Henrietta wasn't too sure about them at first. She glared at them, but then suddenly they were behind her. I don't think Henrietta did that. I haven't seen her float Aqui or Alli yet, although I'm afraid she tried a few times.

Aqui and Alli can get out of Roadrunner's way when she's charging toward them.

Buffy was too busy dust-bathing in Henrietta's favorite spot to be interested in new chickens.

I don't know where Chameleon is (maybe she's hiding from the new chickens?).

Freckles, Speckles, and Chatterbox (my Speckled Sussex hens) crowded around Aqui and Alli, and even though they didn't try to peck them or anything, Aqui and Alli got out of their way in a hurry.

Unusual abilities:
I think they can teleport. Chris thinks so too.

Needs further research:
Chris says we should measure how far they can go,

and if they can go farther if they practice, or when they're older.

Can they teleport through things, or just through air? (Chris thinks Hortensia sent them in a cage so they couldn't teleport out of their crate, and I agree, but we haven't tested it yet.)

Can they do anything else?

Note: Check out The Hoboken Chicken Emergency from the library again, because Aquí and Allí haven't heard it yet.

Date: Sunday, August 3
To: Hortensia James <hjames@APeculiarKindofBird.com>
From: Sophie Brown <unusualchickenfarmer@gmail.com>
Subject: RE: RE: New chickens

Dear Hortensia,

I don't have any roosters. I need to figure out where my incubator is, though. Can you send the eggs next week instead?

Sincerely,
Sophie

PS Agnes trusted me to do a good job, so I don't think you need to worry about me and Redwood Farm.

Agnes Taylor

Wherever you believe people go when they die

(you told me you were going, but you forgot to tell me where)

Dear Agnes,

I wish you'd taught me a few more things about chickens. I'm glad you trust me, but I still have a lot to learn. Like how to hatch eggs in an incubator, and whatever else Hortensia thinks I'm supposed to know. I have enough trouble figuring out how to keep Roadrunner from chasing the new chickens, and what to do when Henrietta shuts Buffy out of the henhouse at night. I mean, I try hard, but I've only been a poultry farmer for a couple of months. I can't really blame you, though. It's not your fault you died before I could meet you and be your apprentice, just like it's not Great-Uncle Jim's fault that he died before he could teach me anything about chickens. Besides, if he hadn't left his farm to Dad, I would never have moved here and had chickens at all. And I do love his chickens, even if they don't always do what they're supposed to do.

I bet I would have learned a lot if I had really been your apprentice, though.

Your friend,
Sophie

Mariposa García González

Heaven

Querida Abuelita,

Guess what?!!!??

After Mom got off the phone with Tía Catalina and
Tío Fernando tonight, she said my cousin Lupe is going
to a college near us, and since it costs a lot of money, she
might come stay with us for her first year! When she saw
my happy dance, Mom gave me a big hug and whispered,
"Yo también los extraño." Of course she misses them too.
I wish our farm wasn't so far from LA.

I like my new friends a lot, and I'm getting better at
meeting new people, but it's still pretty hard to introduce
myself and worry that maybe they'll be mean, and hope
I can remember their names and everything. Lupe isn't
my friend exactly, since she's my cousin, and I guess
she's kind of an adult now if she's going to college, but
she still treats me like a friend, even though she's way
older than me.

Te quiero,
Soficita

PS I can teach Lupe how to make migas! She's taught me lots of things, but I've never taught her how to do anything before. I still wish you had taught me how to make them your way, and I bet Lupe does too. But at least I can teach her how to make them my way.

Blackbird Farm

Mariposa García González
Someplace where I'll see you again, eventually

Querida Abuelita,

I told my chickens all about Lupe this morning: how she's the second-oldest of my cousins, and was born in Los Angeles like me and my mom and my aunts and my other cousins, and she lived her whole life in the city till now, so they should be patient with her if she doesn't know much about chickens yet. I told them how she was in the flag troop in high school, and she's Xicana and has curly black hair and brown eyes and brown skin, just like me. I told them that Tía Catalina and Tío Fernando expect them to be a good influence on Lupe, not like those friends of hers who stand around all day near the 7-Eleven, smoking. (Don't worry, Abuelita—Lupe would never smoke. She knows how sick it made you.)

I told my chickens that even though I've known Lupe way longer than I've known them, they shouldn't be jealous. I said they should be nice to her when they meet her, because after all, Lupe doesn't have superpowers like they do. She's more like me: just a regular hardworking person.

17

I haven't decided how much to tell Lupe about my chickens. They're the coolest thing about this farm, so of course she has to meet them. But Lupe doesn't really love Star Wars like I do. I'm not sure what she'll think of a chicken that can use the Force.

Maybe after she gets used to them.

Te quiero,
Soficita

PS I guess opposable thumbs would seem like a great superpower to chickens, since they don't even have hands. And Chameleon's superpower wouldn't seem that cool to a real chameleon. Maybe whether something is super or regular is more about how you look at it.

Date: Monday, August 4
To: Sophie Brown <unusualchickenfarmer@gmail.com>
From: Hortensia James <hjames@APeculiarKindofBird.com>
Subject: RE: RE: RE: New chickens

Dear Sophie,

Sorry, I didn't see your email until after I'd shipped nine eggs to you. Your eggs will arrive tomorrow, so you'd better alert your postal carrier at once, and find that incubator. You absolutely must not keep chicks in with adult chickens, so make sure you have a new area ready for them after they hatch.

Sincerely,
Hortensia

Blackbird Farm

Monday, August 4

Jim Brown
Heaven's Ultimate Chicken Farm, where your favorite
chickens go to rest

Dear Great-Uncle Jim,

I guess I'm going to learn how to hatch chicks. I looked
up what an incubator was in my library books. It's a
plastic or Styrofoam box that you plug in to keep eggs
warm until they hatch.

If you had an incubator, where would you have put it?
I thought maybe in the barn, but I looked and looked and
looked, and didn't find it.

While I was looking through everything, I saw
Gregory from the loft window, so I went down to tell him
that I'm going to get eggs in the mail tomorrow.

I asked if he might know where your incubator was,
since he was your friend, and since I need it right away.
He didn't know, but he said he could meet me and my
dad or mom after work at Agnes's barn and see if we
could find one there, and maybe some chick-raising
information in her file cabinet too.

And you know what? Mom said that Dad would still

be out learning stuff about grapes, but since it was an emergency, she'd take an hour off and come with me and Gregory.

Love,
Sophie

PS Chris has raised chicks before—well, Buffy hatched them for him, really, so he didn't have to use an incubator, and then his Polish chicks came in the mail already hatched, so he didn't do that part. But they were only a day old when they got here in their box, so he said he'd help me raise them. Samantha hasn't ever raised chicks, only rabbits, but she says she'll still help. She is very good at making lists and figuring out what to do.

PPS Chris says maybe the new chicks could live at Redwood Farm, since Agnes probably had lots of chicken areas.

PPPS The chickens you left for me send their love. I know they miss you. Even Henrietta.

Blackbird Farm

Monday, August 4

Jim Brown
Chicken Valhalla (where brave chickens go to sing
songs of their slug-vanquishing days and eat all the stale
hot dog buns they ever wanted)

Dear Great-Uncle Jim,

I was really excited to visit Redwood Farm and find a
place for my new chicks to live after they hatch. Agnes
had a lot of chicken coops, and they're really neat—
each coop has an outdoor cage called a chicken run,
with the henhouse inside, kind of like for zoo animals.
I guess because Agnes had a lot of kinds of chickens that
couldn't all be together, so they couldn't just come out
of the henhouse and run around the barnyard, like my
chickens.

But it looks like it's going to be a lot of work to get the
chicken coops ready for my chicks.

I know Agnes did her best, but Gregory said when she
got older, it was hard for her to keep up with things. He
said he should have helped more, but he didn't know how
much she needed it. Mom told him that sometimes letting
people decide how they want to do things shows respect

too, even if it would be easier on you to just help them. He agreed, but his face said he was still sad about it.

Gregory says I'll need my gloves for the blackberry brambles and the poison oak that are filling up the chicken runs, and Mom says it will be hard work, especially when it's so hot out. But my chickens are worth it.

At least there aren't any blackberry brambles in the barn. There's a desk with a box marked "Outbox" and a filing cabinet in one corner. There's a bunch of wood shavings on the floor. And on the other walls, there are boxes and trash cans and some tools and lumber and stuff that I don't even know what it is.

Gregory explained that since Agnes left Redwood Farm to me, everything in here was mine now, so I could look at whatever I wanted and even take it home. Mom asked if she could look through the filing cabinet and see if there were any instructions that might help me. I told her sure.

Gregory and I made a list of what I'll need to incubate eggs and hatch chicks:

1. An incubator
2. Sterilizing solution for the incubator
3. A thermometer
4. A hygrometer (to measure humidity)
5. A chick brooder, for after the chicks hatch
6. A heat lamp, to keep the chicks warm

7. A chick waterer
8. A chick feeder
9. Chick food (Gregory says this has special medicine in it—it isn't just regular chicken food put through a blender or something)
10. Chick grit (very, very small rocks— even chicks eat rocks!)

"That's a long list of things," I told him. Gregory knows we don't have a lot of money for stuff like this. He nodded, serious. "This isn't a beginning chicken project. But if we don't find it all here, you might be able to borrow what you need from me, or another farmer."

I nodded. "Okay."

"Just keep your eyes open for that incubator," he told me. "Let me know when you find something that might be it."

So I took one wall, and he took another. I started reading the labels on all the boxes. ROW COVER, PLANT STAKES & TAGS, 4-INCH POTS, RABBIT & SUET FEEDERS, GRIT.

"Aha!" I said. I had to move a bunch of other boxes to be able to open the box that said GRIT.

Sure enough, there was a plastic bag inside that said CHICK GRIT, along with some others that just said POULTRY GRIT.

Gregory came over and felt the weight of the bag. He said that should be enough.

I made a big check mark on the list.

"Soficita, come see if this is helpful," Mom said.

I went over to look.

REDWOOD FARM SUPPLY INCUBATION CHECKLIST.

Instructions! "Nice work, Mom," I told her. She said she'd hang on to them and would look for anything else that might help me.

Gregory said the thermometer and hygrometer he found on the windowsill would work, once I'd cleaned the dust off. Two more check marks!

I found chick food in a metal garbage can. (What is it with these Gravenstein farmers keeping food in trash cans??) The label was taped to the bottom of the lid, so Gregory read it to make sure it was right for chicks. He said it was, so I checked that off the list too.

"Well, the good news is, you've got yourself an incubator now," Gregory told me, showing me a big Styrofoam box with a plug coming out of it.

"What's the bad news?" I asked.

"The bad news is, it isn't the kind that's easy to use."

Gregory handed the incubator to me.

"Where's the on/off switch?" I asked.

Gregory laughed. "This one doesn't have anything fancy like that," he said. "You just plug it in."

I frowned. "Then how can it be hard to use?"

Smiling, he shook his head. "It isn't hard to make

it work; it's only hard to keep the temperature right to hatch your chicks. You have to remember to check on it a few times a day, and turn it up or down a tiny bit when you need to." He showed me the dial that said "Increase" and "Decrease."

"I can add it to my chicken-chores list," I told him.

Gregory nodded. "Good plan."

I took the lid off the incubator. Inside, there was a bottle labeled "Ultra-Cleen Hatching Solution," a plastic bottle with a tray stuck to it, a metal tray with a weird lid with holes in it, and some sticks. I examined the sticks. They were about a foot and a half long, narrow and a little bumpy.

I showed him what was in the box.

"Sterilizer, chick feeder, chick waterer, and chick roosts," Gregory told me. "Good find."

I marked them off the list. I didn't tell him that at first I thought maybe I'd found a batch of magic wands. They weren't fancy, not like the Harry Potter ones, but then Agnes's farm wasn't exactly Hogwarts either.

Then Gregory found a metal light in a box under where the incubator had been. It had a red lightbulb. "Here's your heat lamp," he said, showing it to me.

"All that's left is a chick brooder," I told him.

He nodded. "You'll have time to figure that part out— that's where the chicks will live after they hatch. People even make them out of cardboard boxes." He looked at the pile of stuff we'd gathered up. "I think you're all set. Let's get all this in your car."

Now I just have to read my instructions and set everything up for my new eggs!

Love,
Sophie

PS I wonder what kind of superpowers they'll have?

PPS You know what Agnes had? One of those fancy chicken waterers, like at the feedstore! I brought it home and cleaned it up. My chickens love it so much!

PPPS Mom found a quiz and a catalog at Redwood Farm too. I didn't think it would be cheating to read it. It doesn't list superpowers.

REDWOOD FARM QUIZ:
ARE YOU READY TO HATCH EGGS?

This quiz must be completed and submitted to Redwood Farm before ordering fertile hatching eggs. You must answer all questions in order to score the quiz effectively.
Be accurate and honest. We will know.

1. Do you have suitable homes ready for any and all chicks you hatch?

A) That's someone else's problem.

(B)) Yes, I have space for all of them on my farm—even if they're all roosters.

C) I'm going to build them a replica of the Empire State Building out of cardboard boxes. It should be ready in about ten years.

D) My pet boa constrictor's stomach is ready.

2. Do you have a stable location for your incubator that's near a power outlet, away from predators (including dogs, cats, and rats), out of direct sunlight, in a reasonable temperature range (approximately 65–85 degrees F)?

A) I'll just put the eggs in the refrigerator until they hatch.

(B)) Yes, my incubator is clean and ready. *almost* I should be okay unless the power goes out or there's some really weird weather.

C) Sure, I'll go to the zoo, pretend to be a zookeeper, and set everything up in their special behind-the-scenes area. No one will see through my disguise.

D) My pet boa constrictor will keep them nice and warm.

3. Are you prepared to check the temperature and humidity in the incubator and carefully turn the eggs at least 2–3 times per day, every day, for the next 16–18 days?

    A) Someone else will do all that boring stuff.

    B) Yes, I'll add it to my farm chores, even if it means I have to visit my classroom on the weekends or say no to friends who are planning fun trips.

    C) Well, not tomorrow—I have to climb Mount Everest. And the day after that I have an Olympic-level fencing match.

    D) If it's good enough for my boa, it's good enough for these eggs.

4. Will you have your brooder ready in a predator-free place for all the chicks that hatch, complete with a heat lamp, chick feeder, chick waterer, and medicated chick food?

    A) Whatever.

    B) Yes, I'll be ready. I'm committed to doing my best for these chicks.

    C) Tell the postal worker to leave the box anywhere. I'm out of town.

    D) That . . . won't be necessary.

How to score your quiz:

Give yourself:

1 point for each A

3 points for each B

2 points for each C

0 points for each D

12 points: Ready to Hatch

You think you're ready, but hatching chicks will be harder than you think. Still, I believe you can do it. You may now order fertile hatching eggs from Redwood Farm Supply.

8–11 points: Only in Your Dreams
You like the idea of hatching eggs more than you'd like the reality. Write a story about it instead, or help someone else with their incubation project. Feel free to take this quiz again if you decide you really do want to do this.

4–7 points: Just Bored
You don't really want to hatch eggs—or you don't want to do the work it takes to hatch eggs. Find another science fair project, hobby, or career. Please give this attached note to your parent/teacher/employer:

Regretfully, Redwood Farm Supply has encountered an error that cannot be rectified, and we are unable to ship fertile hatching eggs to this customer.

0–3 points: Exceptional Herpetologist (Stay Away from Unusual Chickens)
Though your devotion to your boa constrictor is admirable, the unusual chickens from Redwood Farm Supply would not be a safe or suitable meal for it. (Trust us.) Wouldn't you rather hatch reptile eggs? Write to Sun & Sand Herpetology to learn more.

REDWOOD FARM SUPPLY
INCUBATION CHECKLIST

Congratulations on purchasing fertile hatching eggs from Redwood Farm Supply!

PART ONE

To set up your incubator and prepare your new eggs:

Clean your incubator with soap and water.

Clean the plastic liner of your incubator with an appropriate disinfectant.

Assemble your incubator per its instructions.

Place your incubator where you can safely hatch your eggs. (You won't want to move it after the eggs are inside.)

Fill any channels with water to maintain humidity. (See your incubator's instruction manual.)

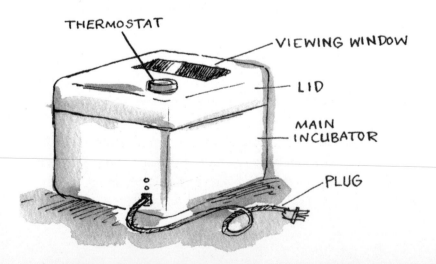

THERMOSTAT
VIEWING WINDOW
LID
MAIN INCUBATOR
PLUG

Plug in your incubator.

Adjust the thermostat using the dial on the lid to increase or decrease the temperature, or according to your incubator's instruction manual.

Place your thermometer and hygrometer inside the incubator, where you'll be able to read them through the window in the incubator's lid.

Put the lid back on the incubator.

Wash your hands. (Always make sure your hands are clean before handling fertile hatching eggs!)

Unwrap your eggs and mark each egg with an X on one long side and an O on the opposite long side.

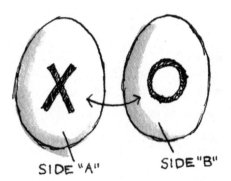

SIDE "A"   SIDE "B"

Carefully place the eggs in a clean egg carton, big round end up.

Let the eggs sit undisturbed at room temperature for 12–24 hours. This allows the air sacs inside to stabilize and move back to the big end, if they were shaken up during shipping.

To begin incubating your eggs:

Check the incubator's thermometer. If the temperature isn't 99.5 degrees F, adjust the thermostat dial. Do not put the eggs inside until the temperature is correct.

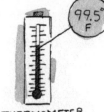

THERMOMETER

Check the incubator's hygrometer. If the humidity isn't between 45% and 55%, add or remove water from the channels. Do not put the eggs inside until the humidity is correct.

HYGROMETER

Wash your hands.

Carefully place the eggs on their sides in the incubator, like they're lying down. Turn all the eggs so you can see the X.

Put the lid back on the incubator.

Check the temperature, but don't turn it up! Instead, check it again after 4–6 hours—if it's still too low, you can adjust it then. Adding room-temperature eggs will lower the temperature at first, but you don't want to accidentally cook them by raising the temperature too high.

Be sure to complete the following tasks at least 2–3 times every day (5 times is better), for Days 1–18 for standard chicken eggs (Days 1–15 for bantam chicken eggs):

Wash your hands.

Check the temperature inside the incubator. If it does not read 99.5 degrees F, adjust the thermostat dial accordingly.

Check the humidity inside the incubator. If it is close to or below 45%, add more water to the channels. If it is close to or above 55%, mop up some water or tape some plastic wrap partway over the channels.

Open the incubator and turn the eggs so that the opposite marking shows on all eggs.

Put the lid back on the incubator.

Note: It is extremely rare for all eggs to hatch and for all chicks to survive hatching. As a responsible poultry keeper, you will provide the best possible chance for your eggs to hatch and your chicks to thrive by following these instructions. If you've done everything you could, please know it isn't your fault if something goes wrong.

For Days 19–21 for standard chicken eggs (Days 16–21 for bantam chicken eggs), see REDWOOD FARM SUPPLY INCUBATION CHECKLIST, Part Two.

Date: Tuesday, August 5
To: Hortensia James <hjames@APeculiarKindofBird.com>
From: Sophie Brown <unusualchickenfarmer@gmail.com>
Subject: Eggs to hatch

Dear Hortensia,

Thank you very much for the eggs. Most of them made it here just fine, except for two. That wasn't Gregory's fault, and I guess it probably wasn't your mailman's fault either.

I will let you know when the rest of the eggs hatch.

Sincerely,
Sophie

PS My friend Chris says they look like bantam eggs, and I agree, so I'm following that schedule. Please tell me if we're wrong.

PPS Don't worry, I'm getting a coop ready for them at Redwood Farm, where they'll have plenty of space away from my other chickens.

Blackbird Farm

Tuesday, August 5

Agnes Taylor

Ghost Farm: ghostly chickens for unusual farmers

Dear Agnes,

Your friend Hortensia sent me some eggs from your chickens. Gregory called us to let us know they arrived, and Dad drove me down to pick them up, and I signed a form for the post office. Dad drove really carefully, and I held the box on my lap the whole time.

Chris came over to see the eggs and help out. I opened the box, and we dug through all the shredded paper and found the eggs, all bubble-wrapped separately. Two of them were broken anyway. I couldn't see any dead chicks inside—Chris says they haven't been around long enough for that—but there was a little blood in the mixed-up raw egg, and I felt like throwing up. But Chris said we needed to concentrate on taking care of the rest of them, so I just kept moving.

We unwrapped all the eggs that weren't broken, and Chris put them in an egg carton very carefully, big ends up, like you said in your instructions. Chris drew me a calendar while I made a new chore checklist, so I could keep track of the egg tasks as well as all my regular chicken chores. Then we decorated the cardboard box I'm going to use as a brooder. We drew portraits of my other chickens, so the chicks could get to know them while they grow up. (We put Henrietta on the outside of the box, because she might be a little too scary-looking for baby chicks. But I'm sure they'll learn to love her when they're older.)

For some reason your friend Hortensia sent me a plastic bottle too. Chris says it's a different kind of chick waterer, with a metal thing the chicks peck at to make water come out. I'm excited about hatching the eggs, even if I am a little nervous about it.

Your friend,
Sophie

PS Gregory told me that farmers almost never ship adult chickens, only eggs or just-hatched chicks. That's why Hortensia sent the other chickens special delivery instead of to the post office.

PPS I didn't tell him I thought it would be a bad idea to ship eggs or chicks like Aquí and Allí that were small enough to fit through the wire cage Hortensia sent them in, even if it was in a crate too. I guess sometimes you have to make different arrangements for unusual chickens.

Agnes Taylor

Heaven's Best Hatchery

Dear Agnes,

I'm incubating your eggs now. Just thought you'd like to know. It was pretty tough to get the temperature just right, with only a dial that says "Increase" and "Decrease." But I was patient and tried not to get too frustrated.

Now I just need to wait. For days and days and days. And turn the eggs. Over and over and over and over again.

Good thing I have Great-Uncle Jim's chickens and Aquí and Allí to keep me busy until they hatch.

Your friend,

Sophie

PS I'm going to practice observing Great-Uncle Jim's chickens as well as Aquí and Allí. After all, they're from Redwood Farm too.

Sophie's Chicken & Egg Chores:

Morning:

Wash hands
Check temperature and humidity
Turn eggs
Feed chickens & give them clean water
Collect eggs
Make sure no one's being too mean to Aquí and Allí

Afternoon:

Wash hands
Check temperature and humidity
Turn eggs
Clean poop out of the henhouse
Give my chickens a treat
Read to my chickens
Record chicken-observation notes
Sell Henrietta's glass eggs to the feedstore
Buy more chicken food with my glass-egg money

Night:

Wash hands
Check temperature and humidity
Turn eggs
Check to make sure Henrietta didn't lock any of the
   chickens out of the henhouse for the night

Poultry breed observations by: Sophie Brown, unusual poultry farmer

Observations made: Thursday, August 7

Type of bird: Bantam White Leghorn

Gender of bird: Hen (like Henrietta, get it?!?)

PLEASE RECORD YOUR NOTES ABOUT THE FOLLOWING:

Comb: pinkish red and pointy

Beak: yellow and pointy

Eyes: orange with black pupils

Wattles: red

Earlobes: white

Beard: nope

Head: white

Neck: white

Body: white

Tail: white, points up

Legs and Feet: yellow, no feathers

Eggs: bantam-size eggs that look and feel like glass (not edible)

Typical movements: Walks around, glares at everyone, moves other chickens out of her way, opens and closes the henhouse door with her mind.

comb

earlobe

Grrrr!

beak

wattle

Typical vocalizations (if any): Kind of loud and a little cranky

Interactions with other poultry: Everyone knows Henrietta is the top chicken, even Aquí and Allí, so they don't bother her too much.

Unusual abilities: Henrietta can move things with the power of her little chicken brain. Even things that are bigger than she is.

Needs further research: What's the biggest thing she can move? (Note: test this carefully!!!)

Blackbird Farm

Friday, August 8

Mariposa García González

A place where you're happy, even if we miss you

Querida Abuelita,

Guess what? LUPE IS FINALLY HERE!!!

When Samantha called this morning to see if I could go blackberry picking, Mom told me to go ahead, everything was ready for Lupe, and if I brought enough blackberries home, we could make something special for dessert. Dad thought she'd probably be here by dinner, if traffic wasn't too bad.

Samantha told me to wear sunglasses and long sleeves and pants, and to bring a bucket and a wire coat hanger.

Dad helped me find a bucket and a coat hanger, and Mom suggested I take peanut butter and pickle sandwiches and apples. I made peanut butter and jelly instead, because even though peanut butter and pickle is my mom's favorite and I kind of like them too, I don't eat them in public.

Everything fit in the bucket, even my water bottle. I hung it on my bike handlebar and rode off to meet Samantha by the trail.

The only person we saw for the first mile of trail was a teenage white girl on a horse who waved to us. I never knew you had to wear a special helmet when you rode a horse. Sam says otherwise you could fly off and land on your head and kill yourself, just like you could riding a bike. I wanted to know why they didn't make one helmet for riding bikes and horses and maybe motorcycles, so you didn't have to have so many different helmets. "Maybe they do," she said. "Or, maybe no one does yet, so you could invent them and make a million dollars when you grow up."

But I reminded her that I was going to be a poultry farmer and sell chickens to people, so I wasn't really going to have time for that.

Finally, Sam stopped near some huge blackberry bushes. She got out a blanket and spread it on the ground, and I collapsed onto it. "Lunch first!" I said.

So we had a picnic. Sam brought sandwiches with something called braunschweiger, with lettuce and pickle. It was a ground-up spread that smelled kind of good but weird. "What is it?" I asked her.

She thought about it for a moment. "I don't really know. Maybe ground-up liver or something? It's kind of like spreadable hot dogs."

I tried one. It was pretty good, whatever it was. She said her mom was going to make sardine sandwiches, but Sam didn't know if I was okay with eating fish with the bones and eyeballs still in it, and besides, they got smelly on hot days.

After lunch, Sam showed me how to unwrap the wire on the coat hanger, straighten it out so it's long enough, and pull the tall vines down with the hook, because the best berries are too high to reach. Her grandfather showed her how.

Sam said her mom calls the trail people every year to make sure they haven't been sprayed with any bad chemicals, even though every year the trail people tell her they're not allowed to spray, since it's bad for the creek. She says you shouldn't pick the ones that are low enough for a dog to pee on, though. I asked about horses, because they're taller than dogs, but Sam has never seen a horse pee on blackberry bushes, so she thinks we're okay, as long as we wash them off well.

"What will you do with all your blackberries?" I asked after we'd been picking for more than an hour.

"Most of them get washed and then go in the freezer for later," Sam told me. "So you can have blackberries whenever you want them. But if I bring home at least half a bucket, Mom will make pie too. Or Dad will make crisp, because he isn't good at piecrust, but he knows how to do the crunchy topping part. Or you can just eat them with milk and sugar."

It was hot and dusty, but we had our water bottles and sunscreen and sunglasses. That weird summer buzzing

noise went on and on—it's some kind of bug, Dad thinks—
and once in a while a plane would fly overhead, or someone
would walk down the trail and point out any berries we
missed, or ask about the coat hangers. The air smelled a
tiny bit like horse poop, since people don't have to clean up
after horses the way they have to clean up after dogs, but
mostly it smelled like sweet hot blackberries.

We ran out of time before we ran out of berries to
pick.

"Maybe I can bring my cousin Lupe next time," I told
her. "She's eighteen, and she's taller than me. And she's
fun."

"Sure," Sam said. "How does she feel about sardines?"

I shrugged. "I can ask her."

Riding home was harder, since I was hot and tired
and had to balance my bucket of blackberries.

But it was worth it when I got home and gave a few
blackberries to my chickens. They loved them so much!
I'm glad, because I'm pretty busy these days, what
with hatching new eggs, and Lupe coming, and school
starting soon. I want them to know they're still the
greatest chickens ever, even if I can't hang out with them
as much.

Then I showed my parents the blackberries and the
crisp recipe I'd written on my arm when Sam called
her dad.

"This is ten times more blackberries than I ever

picked!" Dad told me. "Well—without eating them before we got home, anyway."

Mom grinned. "I hope you ate at least a few!" Then she told me she might need to interview me for an article idea she had about living in the country. "Would you say that blackberry picking is one of the best parts?"

I thought about it. "Well, it's not as good as having chickens, of course. But if you pick blackberries with a friend, and have a picnic, and get to make blackberry crisp for dessert—yeah, I think it's a pretty good part."

Dad was reading the recipe on my arm. "We can do this—no problem!" he told me. He set the oven to 350 degrees and turned it on, and we got to work.

Dad and I have a pretty good routine when we cook together. First, we decide who's going to be the boss chef and who's going to be the sous-chef, who's more like the chef's assistant. Since I picked the blackberries, we agreed I'd be the boss chef this time.

Meanwhile, Mom set the table for four, and put Lupe's favorite pasta salad in our most beautiful bowl, and got out chips and corn salsa that she'd made from the corn and tomatoes and cilantro that Jane gave us from their garden, and some pickled jicama that Gregory gave us when he heard my cousin was coming to stay with us.

Once the blackberry crisp was baking in the oven, we waited and waited and I got antsy, and finally Dad put some music on. Then we danced to Beyoncé with the music so loud we almost didn't hear Lupe at the door. You can turn the music up really loud when you have a whole house, and nobody bangs on your ceiling or anything!

But somehow Mom heard the doorbell, and Lupe came in and put a huge bunch of flowers on the table and danced with us and gave us all the hugs and kisses that everyone from LA had sent for us. She'd changed her hair since we moved away—it's short-curly now, instead of long-curly—and she was wearing jeans and a skater sweatshirt with flowers and a dragon on it. But she still has the same smile. Mom made us stand next to each other to see who's taller (Lupe, but not by much now!). Then Mom hugged us and told us what beautiful, smart, strong young women we are, and cried a little bit, but in a good way. Like you used to.

We miss you, of course, and we always will. But we know you would want us to have fun, and we're doing a good job of it.

Te quiero,
Soficita

PS You know what? That blackberry crisp was the best we'd ever had in our whole lives, even though it was the first time I made one. I'm going to pick blackberries every year!

SAM'S DAD'S BLACKBERRY CRISP RECIPE
(AS WRITTEN ON MY ARM)

Ingredients:

- 4 cups blackberries, fresh or frozen (enough to cover the bottom of a casserole dish)
- 1 tablespoon cornstarch
- ½ cup flour
- 1 cup brown sugar
- 1 cup oats
- ½ cup (1 stick) butter

Instructions:

1. Preheat oven to 350 degrees.

2. Put the blackberries in the pan.

3. Sprinkle the cornstarch over the blackberries and stir them around. (This step doesn't have to be perfect. In fact, Sam says her dad doesn't worry about getting any of it perfect, and it still tastes great every time!)

4. Cut up the butter into chunks and put it in a bowl with the flour, brown sugar, and oats.

5. Squish the butter into all the rest of the stuff and mix everything with your (clean!) fingers, until it feels like little floury, oaty butter lumps.

6. Carefully dump the lumps all over the top of the blackberries. Spread them out evenly.

7. Bake in the oven for about 30–40 minutes, or until the blackberries look more like jam and the lumps are medium brown and the whole thing smells amazing.

8. If you have any left over, put some tinfoil over it and put it in the fridge.

Note: Sam says you can make crisp with pretty much any fruit, not just blackberries. Although she's never heard of anyone making banana or pineapple crisp.

Blackbird Farm

Saturday, August 9

Mariposa García González
Heaven

Querida Abuelita,

Today I woke up when the birds started singing, and
I couldn't go back to sleep. So I snuck downstairs very
quietly and made myself some oatmeal.

It wasn't long until Lupe came down. Once she'd
eaten her oatmeal and made some coffee for her travel
mug, I told her I'd show her around.

It was a perfect morning. I mean, it's summer, so
everything is dry and brown and dusty, but it wasn't too
hot yet, and Dad borrowed Gregory's friend Mark's goats
the other day to do a lot of cleaning up. (Mom took a
picture of Dad walking the goats on leashes. Everyone in
LA was amazed!)

We still have all of Great-Uncle Jim's junk piles, of
course, but I explained to Lupe that they weren't just
junk, they were junk that he thought he might need, and
that a lot of farmers keep a lot of things around just in
case. Violet says that's from when there weren't many
stores in town, and that farmers can't always afford to
buy things right when they need them.

Lupe loved our barn. I explained about the incubator and my new eggs, and how I have to keep them the same temperature that the mom hen's fluffy feathers would keep them, and I have to turn them the way she would, so the chick embryos develop properly in their eggs. I can't let the humidity get too high, or the eggs won't lose enough moisture, so there won't be enough space for air for the chick embryos to breathe. I can't let it get too low either, or the eggs will dry out and the chicks could get stuck to their shells when they try to hatch.

Lupe is really excited to learn to use Great-Uncle Jim's old typewriter in the barn loft. She got the paper in almost straight on her first try, and I can tell she'll do great, with a little more practice.

From the window, I saw Gregory driving up the road, so we ran down to see him. I told him that his pickled jicama was great, and he asked Lupe when her school starts, and reminded me that we don't have any 4-H meetings this month, because of vacations and school starting. Then he had to go deliver the mail, so we let him get back to work.

When we went to see my chickens, Buffy came right up to say hello, and she even let Lupe pet her! Lupe says we should make her a Chicken Award for being so brave, like the student awards at school. Speckles had just laid an egg, so she and Freckles and Chatterbox all had to bawk about it for a while, and even Henrietta joined in. Chameleon, Roadrunner, Aquí, and Allí were all rolling around in the dust, taking dust baths. They made Lupe laugh so hard!! I'm glad Aquí and Allí are making friends here. I think it would be okay if we came back later to hang out with them for a while. After all, Henrietta's never floated a person. At least, not that I know of.

Then Lupe drove us into town. She couldn't look at everything I pointed out, because she had to pay attention to the road. She's not used to cow-crossing signs and tractors and narrow roads without lanes yet. But we got there.

Lupe loved the feedstore, even though they don't have any chicks right now. Jane showed us a new kind of chicken treat she'd just gotten in, some kind of dried bug. She gave me a sample so I could try it with my chickens and let her know what they thought. "If they like it, maybe we could make a sign so other people know what real chickens think," she told me. That kind of thing can be really helpful.

Lupe stared at the dried-up bugs in the little bag. They were shiny black, and some of their legs had gotten broken off. "These are really gross and really cool," she said.

"You know, if you were making a birthday cake for a chicken, you could use those legs as sprinkles," I told Lupe and Jane.

Lupe shivered. "I'm glad I'm not a chicken!"

Then we went to the library to get Lupe a library card.

As soon as we walked in, Ms. O'Malley took one look at us and said, "Thank heavens!"

It turned out the teen book club had just finished their books and pizza, but a lot of them were on vacation, and Ms. O'Malley was stuck with a whole extra pizza that wouldn't fit in the library refrigerator. "Do you think you could each eat two pieces?" she asked us. "It's mushroom and olive."

We agreed to help her out, since that's what a good neighbor does. It was still kind of warm, even! While we ate, Ms. O'Malley gave Lupe the library-card form and got her set up. "What will you be studying?" she asked when she found out Lupe was going to college here.

"I'm not sure yet, but I think I might study education, so I could be a teacher," Lupe told her.

I never knew Lupe might want to be a teacher. I didn't even know to ask what she was going to college for. I thought you went to college first and then became whatever you want to be later.

"Good choice!" Ms. O'Malley said, handing Lupe her card. "Sophie, our replacement copy of Love, Ruby Lavender came in. You might like it—it has chickens."

So I said I'd give it a try and checked it out. She also found me a book with a little bit about the science of hatching eggs. Ms. O'Malley always tries to be helpful.

"How's the ice cream?" Lupe nodded at the ice cream store as we left the library.

I shrugged. "I didn't bring any money," I told her. I didn't want to tell her I'd never been to the ice cream place because we didn't really have money for that.

"My treat!" she said, grinning.

So we went into the ice cream store. It was small, with ice cream colors everywhere—mint chip tables and Neapolitan chairs and vanilla lights that looked like sundaes, and a white lady in a rainbow sherbet apron.

Lupe got coffee crackle chocolate dream. I decided on chocolate peanut butter.

Lupe paid, and I picked a table.

"How do you like living here now?" Lupe asked me as she licked her ice cream into a smooth dome.

I thought about it as I pushed the ice cream down onto the cone with my tongue so it would stick better. "I still miss LA," I told her. "And all of you—well, until you got here. But it's better here now that I have some friends, and I couldn't have chickens in LA."

Lupe nodded. We licked our ice creams in silence for a little while.

Then Lupe crunched her cone really loudly, and I laughed.

"What's next?" she asked.

I hesitated. Redwood Farm Supply was hard to

explain. But I really wanted her to see it. "Did you hear I inherited a chicken company?"

(I have to go teach Lupe how to make migas now. But don't worry, I'll come back after dinner and tell you all about the rest of our day.)

Later:

We made the best migas ever tonight!! You would have loved them. Now, back to our day.

Lupe and I almost got lost getting to Redwood Farm, but we figured it out. Lupe was very quiet when she got out of the car. I tried to look at Agnes's farm through her eyes.

Great-Uncle Jim's farm has a lot of junk, and there are still some weeds and blackberries where Dad and Mark didn't take the goats yet, but there aren't any tarps on the roof to cover up holes or anything. But it also doesn't have a red barn that looks like someone could walk right up and paint a picture of it, or a little white house that the paint is falling off of, with a porch that's covered in some kind of vine.

"It needs some work," I said at last.

Lupe looked at me. "It's beautiful," she said, and I could tell she really meant it.

I got out my key and led her up the path, past the overgrown flowers, to the barn.

After I'd showed her all the boxes of chicken stuff,

and then the chicken pens that were still full of blackberry brambles, Lupe wanted to see the house.

I hesitated. "I haven't really gone in there yet."

"Then we don't have to. It's up to you, chicken-company owner," Lupe said, smiling.

But I could tell she wanted to see it. And what was I waiting for, anyway? It wasn't going to be more mine next week. I just . . . Since I hadn't been inside, maybe I could imagine Agnes still living there. Maybe I could meet her someday.

But that wasn't true, and I knew it. "We can go in," I told Lupe.

We were careful of the porch, in case it might fall down. My key worked on the front door, just like Gregory said it would.

Agnes's house had lots of windows, and that feeling there's no one around, not like apartments, where you can always hear some neighbor. It wasn't stacked high with stuff, like Great-Uncle Jim's, and the furniture was kind of old, but still pretty.

"This is amazing," Lupe said, looking at a blue bowl on the wooden table in the kitchen. "All this is yours?" She opened a cupboard door, and it was full of jars of jam and peanut butter and cans of food.

"I guess," I said. "I'm still getting used to the idea."

All the rooms were set up like someone was living there, but no one was. Agnes's lawyers said the electricity and water and stuff was already paid for a year, so at least we didn't have to worry about that yet. The beds had sheets on them and faded scratchy blankets with silky edges, and there was soap hanging from a magnet-hook in the bathroom over the sink. There was even still shampoo. I started walking faster, the more rooms we went into, and Lupe didn't say anything when I went past a door without opening it and back into the living room.

"We need to get home before Violet leaves, so you can meet her," I told Lupe.

She nodded. "Okay."

I started to feel a little better once we were back in the car. It was really nice that Agnes left me her company and farm and everything. I don't know why it makes me feel weird sometimes.

"So, tell me about Violet," Lupe said.

So I told her how Violet is Jane's girlfriend who grew up on a farm, but she works for a bank now, at least during the day. She's black, like Gregory, and when she farms, she wears her old jeans, with her braids all wrapped up in a beautiful orange scarf that would look just as good with her fancy gray bank suit. "She and Jane have a fruit and vegetable farm, but they both have other work to do too," I told Lupe.

Lupe nodded. "Do a lot of farmers have other jobs?"

"Yeah, I guess so," I told her. "Ms. O'Malley works for the library, and she has chickens, and Gregory delivers the mail—he has Call ducks, not chickens. But Chris's mom just has a farm, with a vegetable stand and a U-pick apple orchard."

"Maybe it's hard to make a living farming these days," Lupe said.

I shrugged. "Maybe." I hoped not, though, because it was all Dad had right now. Mom's been writing all kinds of articles, but I knew things were still pretty tough since Dad lost his job.

Violet was helping Dad when we got back to the farm, so Lupe got to meet her. Lupe loved Violet's gorgeous bronze nail polish, and it turned out Violet went to Lupe's college, so Violet gave her some tips. "You're going to do great there," Violet said, squeezing Lupe's arm, and Lupe suddenly looked a lot happier. Maybe even Lupe is a little nervous about starting school.

Then Violet told me her friend Cindy is teaching science at my new school, and that I should tell her Violet says to say hi. I told her I would do that.

Violet and Dad had to get back to the grapes then, and Lupe needed to figure out how to register for her classes, and I had to do all my egg and chicken chores and observations, and write to you.

I can tell Lupe really likes it here.

Te extraño,
Soficita

PS What would you have done with all the zucchini that Joy keeps giving Mom? Did you ever put zucchini in migas? I tried giving a huge zucchini to my chickens, but they don't seem to know it's food.

MY CHICKENS' FAVORITE TREATS!

I gave some of these dried bugs to my chickens. They like them even better than sunflower seeds!

Warning: your chickens might love them so much they get rowdy with each other, all trying to get the most treats. (Mine did.)

Sophie Brown, poultry farmer

Redwood Farm

Saturday, August 9

Blackbird Farm

Sunday, August 10

Jim Brown
Farmhalla

Dear Great-Uncle Jim,

Do you need to be patient to be a good farmer? I guess
you probably are, or you'd be the kind of ghost that goes
around throwing things, since you can't do anything
else about what's happening on your farm now. Thank
you for being patient.

I'm still excited about hatching my eggs, but it sure
takes a long time to do it. And a whole lot of reading
thermometers and hygrometers and very carefully
turning eggs. No wonder kids at my old school start with
bean plants instead.

I wonder what kind of chickens they'll grow up to be?
Maybe they'll lay golden eggs, so Dad can stop doing all
those interviews and Mom can finally write her novel,
and maybe we could get a family computer instead of
me having to wait until Mom is done working to send
an email. But if we start taking gold eggs to the bank,
someone's going to want to steal my chickens again.

Maybe they could be like metal detectors instead,

and just find everyone's lost change and jewelry. Enough to help out, but not so much that someone would steal them instead of just buying a metal detector.

I'll let you know in about thirteen days.

Love,
Sophie

PS I hope I don't have a bunch of little Henriettas running around trying to figure out their powers. Don't get me wrong, I love Henrietta! But I'm not nearly as patient as Yoda, and I don't want any of them going to the Dark Side because I didn't notice they were having issues.

PPS I think Aquí and Allí are Blue Copper Marans. They're in the old Redwood Farm catalog Mom found, but it doesn't say what their powers are. I already figured that out, though.

Blue Copper Marans

Standard height, blue plumage with copper hackles, lightly feathered legs and feet. Red evenly serrated single comb, red earlobes.

Large dark brown eggs, frequent layer. Easily distracted with treats.

Blackbird Farm

Monday, August 11

Mariposa García González
Someplace where people respect each other

Querida Abuelita,

Lupe and I visited our new schools today, so we could
figure out where things were before we had to hurry up
and try to get to class on time.

The whole way to my school, Lupe told me how much
I was going to love middle school, how I could finally be
in the flag troop, like she was, or on the soccer team, like
her brother Javier was, or even both.

When we lived in LA, I could picture myself at Cesar
Chavez Junior High, because I visited it when Javier and
Lupe went there. I never worried about sticking out in a
big school full of brown kids. But my new middle school
is so small I don't know if they'll even have a flag team,
and I haven't met anyone here that looks like me. I bet
everyone will know right away that I'm new.

We didn't sing along with the radio while we drove to
Lupe's school, and Lupe looked pretty nervous when we
drove into the enormous parking lot.

But then we found a big lawn and practiced our

cartwheels. Lupe even taught me one of her flag routines! We peeked through the windows of some classrooms and tiptoed into the library. It's huge and really, really quiet.

We were wondering whether we'd get in trouble if we stuck our feet in the fancy fountain to cool off when a white guy stopped his car in the street and yelled, "Why don't you go back where you came from?" at us.

My stomach twisted and hurt. I grabbed Lupe's hand, and she held on tight. I looked up at her to see what we should do, but she didn't say anything, just stood there, looking like he'd hit her.

It's not like it was the first time I'd heard mean stuff like that. But I still felt scared, and mad, and like throwing up. I used to try to explain that I was born in LA. But it never helped.

At my old school, I didn't like dealing with bullies, but I knew what to do. But who are you supposed to tell when some adult you don't even know is mean to you at college? Should we run away? Tell that guy to stop it? I didn't want Lupe to go to a school where she'd have to listen to stuff like that every day.

Then a white lady with purple spiky hair stopped walking and yelled at the guy that discrimination and harassment are not tolerated on campus and that she was going to report him. She got out her phone and took a picture of his license plate, and he drove off.

The lady hurried over to ask us if we were okay.

"We've heard worse," I told her, even though I was really mad at him for scaring me and ruining Lupe's school visit like that.

"I'm really sorry it happened," the lady told me. "Are you starting this semester?" she asked Lupe.

Lupe nodded. She didn't look excited.

The purple-haired lady wrote something in her notebook, tore it off, and handed it to Lupe. "I'm Kate. Here's my phone number. Call me if you need help finding anything, or you just want to grab some coffee or whatever, okay?"

"Thanks," Lupe said. She still didn't smile, though.

"Are you the class president or something?" I asked Kate.

"No, I'm just a student," she said, smiling. "Hey, I'm on my way to water the garden—want to come?"

I didn't want Lupe to leave her new school still thinking about that guy. "Sure," I told Kate.

The student garden was so cool! Students take care of all the fruits and vegetables, and they pick them to give to people who don't have money for all their own food right now. They even had chickens visiting from a farm, in a special chicken coop! I told Lupe what kinds of chickens I thought they might be, and what they were probably telling each other with all that bawking, and she finally smiled.

By the time we left, she and Kate had a plan to meet up for coffee before class on their first day. Maybe Lupe will like college after all. I hope so.

Te extraño,
Soficita

PS I hope we never see that guy again.

Date: Monday, August 11
To: Sophie Brown <unusualchickenfarmer@gmail.com>
From: Betty Johnson <BJohnson@FluffyChickenHatchery.com>
Subject: Unavoidable delay

Dear Ms. Brown,

I am writing to inform you that it will be at least a month before I can send you fertile eggs from the chickens Agnes left in my care, as these hens are busy helping our local zoo hatch eggs of a very rare species of ibis. I will write to you with an updated timeline as soon as the zoo's eggs have hatched and the chickens are laying again. I do hope you understand.

Sincerely,
Betty

Date: Tuesday, August 12
To: Betty Johnson <BJohnson@FluffyChickenHatchery.com>
From: Sophie Brown <unusualchickenfarmer@gmail.com>
Subject: RE: Unavoidable delay

Dear Betty,

That's fine. My incubator is full of eggs right now, and I'm starting school soon, so even if it takes two months, I won't mind. I'm glad that your chickens could help the zoo out. Let me know when the eggs are ready, and I'll tell Gregory the mailman. He is my 4-H leader, so he's very careful with eggs.

Sincerely,
Sophie

PS It's fine if you just call me Sophie.

PPS I hope these really are chickens, not ibises, and not ibis-chickens. I don't know how to take care of ibises yet.

Blackbird Farm

Tuesday, August 12

Mariposa García González
Someplace where everyone helps each other

Querida Abuelita,

This morning, Lupe helped me check on the eggs and rotate them. The temperature was a little too cold, so I turned it to "Increase" a tiny bit. And I forgot to read the hygrometer before I took off the lid. The humidity was too low, but maybe that was because I opened the incubator? I added some water, just in case.

"I can't wait for your pollitos to hatch!" Lupe said.

I bit my lip. "But I need to have a place for them to live first. I said I'd have a coop ready for them, only . . . I don't know if I can do it all in time. I already have to do all my chicken chores and egg chores, and school's starting soon." I'd been worrying about this since we visited Agnes's farm.

Lupe thought about this, her face serious. Then she smiled. "Maybe you should have a work-party picnic at Redwood Farm."

"But it's not a community center or a church or a school," I told her.

"You can have a work party at any place where there's a bunch of work to do," Lupe said. "You have lots of friends here. Don't you think they'd want to help you get a safe place ready for your new chicks?"

I shrugged. "Everyone's pretty busy."

Lupe gave me a look. "Too busy for a picnic?"

"That's different," I told her.

"No it isn't," Lupe said. "We could have a picnic at your new farm, and we could have tools there in case people felt like doing a little work." She studied my face. "Why don't you want to?"

"I don't want people to see it all messy," I whispered. "What if they think I should have fixed it up by now?"

"Sophie. You're twelve years old. You've owned that farm for what, a month? You are doing the best you can—better than most adults, I bet—but this is a big project. People will see that, and they will want to help. Why shouldn't you let them?"

"I'm almost thirteen," I told her.

"Right," she said. "So you can be in charge of making sandwiches for everyone."

I frowned before I could stop myself.

"What now?" she asked.

"We just . . . we don't have a lot of money right now," I told her.

Lupe nodded, serious. "I know," she said. "But we don't have to do fancy things. And you have a whole pantry of food at your other house that needs to be used before it goes bad. We can make peanut butter and jelly sandwiches, and let people know they're welcome to bring something if they want to." She studied my face. "You don't have to decide now. Just think about it."

I've been thinking about it ever since.

Lupe brought it up again when we were feeding my chickens. "What are the first things that need to happen at the other farm, so you can get things ready for your chicks?"

I sighed. "Well, blackberry bushes grew in the chicken runs, so there's no room for chickens. And some of the wire mesh is coming loose. I'm glad Agnes's friends are sending me eggs, because it's not much of a poultry farm without any chickens, but right now I just have a lot of chicken coops that aren't safe for chickens to live in. And I guess I need to do something about that really big lawn, so the chicks don't get lost in it when they're older and can go outside."

Lupe put her hands on her hips. "Soficita, have you ever mowed a lawn in your life?"

I shrugged.

"Answer the question," she said.

I didn't look at her, but I answered. "No."

She squeezed my hand. "Of course not. You never had a yard until you moved here. Do you know someone who knows how to do it? Or who has a mower?"

I thought about it. "Gregory would know what we need." Lupe didn't say anything, so I thought some more. "Violet would know how to do it. She's helped Dad figure out a lot of things about this farm."

Lupe nodded. "What do you think would have happened if your dad tried to do everything himself?"

I shrugged. "He did try, for a while."

"How'd that work out for him?" Lupe asked.

I sighed. I was remembering Gregory's face when he saw Agnes's farm.

Lupe squeezed my hand again. "I know you want to do everything you can, just like your dad, Soph. But if you know that someone could help, and would want to help, and you don't even ask them—well, are you really doing everything you can for your farm, and for your chicks?"

I didn't answer.

But I know she's going to want to talk about it again. Jane could fix that wire netting better than I could. I hammered some nails in school, but they didn't always turn out like I wanted them to. My chicks will need a safe place to live. But I don't want to see Jane's and Violet's and Ms. O'Malley's faces looking just like Gregory's, all sad because Redwood Farm isn't the way they remembered it.

Te extraño,
Soficita

Blackbird Farm

Tuesday, August 12

Mariposa García González
Heaven

Querida Abuelita,

This afternoon, Chris and Sam came over to meet Lupe.
Chris wanted to see how the eggs were doing, and Sam
told Lupe the way to the drugstore so Lupe could pick
out a new color of nail polish for her first day of school.

After Lupe left, I asked Chris and Sam if they knew
how to mow a really big lawn, like at Agnes's farm.

"Did Agnes have a lawn?" Chris asked. "Or just a
garden and fields?"

"You need a tractor for fields," Sam said.

I know about tractors. Great-Uncle Jim had one, and
Violet has been teaching Dad how to drive it. He doesn't
find it too easy yet.

But Chris was thinking. "A tractor, or sheep, or
maybe goats. Or a riding mower—I bet her front field is
pretty flat. Do you just need to cut the grass, or do you
need it baled?"

I shrugged. I didn't know what baled even was. I bet
Dad doesn't either.

"Can we go see it?" Chris asked.

So we rode to Agnes's farm.

Chris studied the grass. "I think we could cut that with Gregory's riding mower. I helped him cut his grass last summer, so I know how to use it—it isn't hard, not like Jim's big old tractor. And Gregory's friend Mark wanted the grass clippings." He grinned. "You're going to love it, Soph—it's so fun, even if it doesn't go that fast."

"Plus, it's good practice for when you learn to drive a car," Sam said.

Chris and Sam didn't look sad like Gregory. They looked excited. "Can we see the rest?" Chris asked.

"Sure," I said. "Haven't you guys ever been here before? When Agnes was here?"

Chris shook his head as I led them back. "People didn't really visit Redwood Farm. I've never been inside the gate before."

"Why not?" I asked.

Sam thought about that for a moment. "Agnes kept to herself. Everyone knew Redwood Farm was special."

I nodded.

"She should have let people come, though," Chris said. "My mom would have helped weed her garden, or made me do it. It wouldn't have been that bad. And I bet my mom would have loved some cuttings from her plants for our garden." He examined the chicken coops. "These are amazing. I wish I could have seen them when all her chickens were here."

I looked at them too. Agnes left me her farm. She'd want those coops filled up with chickens again. I tried to imagine a whole coop full of Roadrunners, or Henriettas—enough that Chris and Sam could have unusual chickens too. If unusual chickens were right for them, of course.

"Those apples will be ripe any day." Sam pointed to an enormous tree. "They're Gravensteins, my mom's favorites."

I looked at the tree. There were enough apples for an entire town on that tree. "How do you even pick apples that are that high up? Doesn't it take weeks?"

Sam laughed. "You call some friends with apple ladders, who really like Gravensteins. Haven't you ever picked apples before?"

I shook my head. "I'm from LA, remember? What happens if you don't pick them in time?"

Chris shrugged. "They fall off and rot all over the place. Or the deer eat them, if you don't have deer fences."

"Are there deer fences here?" I asked.

Chris shrugged. "We can go look," he said.

So we walked all over the whole farm, around the edge, and Sam and Chris told me that Agnes didn't have any deer fences except for around her flowers and her vegetable garden. We sorted out which blackberry bushes were a problem and which to leave alone for picking. They told me what the fruit trees were, and where the well was.

"How do you know all this?" I asked. "Do you learn it in school?"

Chris shrugged. "This is what people talk about here."

Sam nodded. "Just like you probably know some city stuff."

I thought about that. "Like which bus system uses which kind of transfer, or when the free day is at the museums, or what to do if you see someone getting mugged?"

Chris stared at me. I guess he never learned that stuff.

"Yeah, like that," Sam said.

Too bad none of those things are useful here. But I'm good at learning new things.

Wells: People still use wells here, but not the kind you make a wish in, with the rock circle and the bucket that you wind up. Mostly they look like a metal pipe sticking out of the ground.

We picked a bunch of plums, because Sam said if we didn't they were going to fall off and rot.

"Can you make plum crisp?" I asked.

Sam shrugged. "I don't see why not. You could

even make blackberry-plum crisp if you still have blackberries. There aren't any rules about it."

"Can you put them in the freezer?" I knew we still had space in our freezer, even with all those blackberries.

"Yeah, but it works better if you cut them in half and pull the pits out first," Sam said.

So we made a plan to come back tomorrow to pick more plums.

Te quiero,
Soficita

Poultry breed observations by: Sophie Brown, unusual poultry farmer

Observations made: Tuesday, August 12

Type of bird: Bantam Black Frizzle Cochin

Gender of bird: Hen

PLEASE RECORD YOUR NOTES ABOUT THE FOLLOWING:

Comb: pinkish red, very small, pointy

Beak: gray, pointy

Eyes: orange with black pupils, I think
(Roadrunner doesn't stay still for very long)

Wattles: red

Earlobes: red

Beard: I don't think so, but it's hard to tell, with all those wild feathers

Head: black, looks like she blow-dried her feathers all funny

Neck: black, with feathers in all directions

Body: black, with feathers in all directions

Tail: black, with feathers in all directions

Legs and Feet: covered in wild black feathers

Eggs: light brown eggs, once in a while

Typical movements: Races around the barnyard at top speed; almost never walks anywhere; likes to chase squirrels and charge at other chickens.

Typical vocalizations (if any): Roadrunner's pretty quiet, for a chicken.

Interactions with other poultry: Sometimes the other chickens try to peck Roadrunner, but she can easily outrun them. When she's not in the mood to race around, sometimes she hangs out with Chameleon and Buffy.

Unusual abilities:

Roadrunner runs so fast she just looks like a black blur. But she eats and drinks and flaps her wings and poops and lays eggs the same speed as the other chickens.

Needs further research: Just how fast can Roadrunner run?

Could she run across water if she wanted to?

Can she move her molecules really fast through buildings like the Flash?

Guess not—Henrietta locked her out of the henhouse for almost an hour last night before I found her and put her inside with the others.

Blackbird Farm

Wednesday, August 13

Mariposa García González
Heaven's Best Salon

Querida Abuelita,

Lupe wanted to come pick plums too, so we stopped and
got Chris and Sam and a ladder that Sam's mom said we
could use as long as we locked down the legs and didn't
stand on the top two steps. (Why do they even make
those steps, if they don't want you to stand on them?)
Lupe and I didn't think we could get the ladder into her
Toyota, but Chris and Sam said it would be no problem.
Chris showed us how to wedge it in through the back so
we could hang on to it and keep it from sliding through
the windshield, and made sure Lupe could see out the
front and back and sides clearly around the ladder. Sam
attached bungee cords to keep the back closed, and put
a plastic ribbon on the end of the ladder so other cars
would see it and not crash into it. (You have to do that
here. It's the law.) Then Lupe drove very carefully to
Agnes's farm.

After we got to Agnes's farm and pulled the ladder
out of the car and helped Lupe get back up off the

98

driveway, where she was recovering from the drive, we walked back to the plum tree, and I told Chris and Sam about Lupe's picnic idea.

"That's a really good idea," Sam said.

Chris nodded. "Everyone will want to see Redwood Farm!"

We thought up a list of what people could help with while we picked plums.

"What about cutting the long grass?" I asked.

Chris grinned. "No way! I asked Gregory yesterday, and he said he'd drive his riding mower over tomorrow, after work."

I guess I'm going to mow my first lawn. And have a work-party picnic.

Te quiero,
Soficita

PS Lupe and I painted our fingernails the same color as the plums, a color called Sugar Plum Pie. You would have loved it. She told me how your friend Mrs. Giacomo came and did your nails in the hospital when you were too sick to go to her salon. We miss you a lot.

Potluck Work-Party Picnic
at
Redwood Farm

Saturday, August 16, 11 a.m. to 2 p.m.

Please bring your tools and helpful family and friends! Here's what we need help with:

1. Fix the wire on the chicken runs and make them secure and safe for Sophie's new chicks.

2. Clear the blackberry bushes and other plants out of the chicken runs. (Wear gloves, and look out for poison oak!)

3. Pick Gravenstein apples (not the red ones—they aren't ready yet).

4. Weed garden (if you already know what's a weed and what isn't).

Blackbird Farm

Thursday, August 14

Agnes Taylor
Beyond-the-Grave Chicken Farm

Dear Agnes,

Today Chris and Sam and my cousin Lupe and I mowed your lawn. Gregory's riding mower is SO MUCH FUN!!!

It's like the bumper cars at the theme park, only there isn't anything to run into, and it cuts grass, so it's also getting a useful job done. Chris just drives as fast as he can really close to the trees and stuff, but Sam and Lupe and I made patterns in the grass in case any aliens or astronauts were watching. We wrote, "HI ASTRONAUTS AND EXTRATERRESTRIALS" with the riding mower, and drew some hearts and stars and smiley faces so they would know we were friendly and that we like space too. (Chris said they would think we were in love with them, but I told him no, we love what they do for science, and he should too. You don't have a lot of room to write in a small field, and a heart is a helpful abbreviation.)

No one ran into your house or barn or trees (just one bush, and it'll probably be okay when it grows back,

102

Chris says), and no one broke Gregory's mower, and Mark came and picked up bags and bags of cut grass. He said we could come see his goats anytime.

On our way home, Lupe told me she was really impressed by how many things I've learned to do here.

I love living on a farm.

Your friend,
Sophie

PS We looked in your filing cabinet again and finally found Part Two of your hatching instructions. Phew!

REDWOOD FARM SUPPLY
INCUBATION CHECKLIST

PART TWO

For bantam chicken eggs: *begin Part Two on Day 16. Bantam eggs may hatch as early as Day 18.*

For standard chicken eggs: *set up the incubator for Part Two on Day 19. Standard eggs typically hatch around Day 21.*

Increase the airflow:

> *If your incubator has a fan, make sure it's running.*
> *If your incubator has an air vent, open it at least halfway. Your eggs need airflow as well as humidity at this stage, which can be a difficult balance.*

Check the humidity inside the incubator:

> *If it is close to or below 55%, open the lid and add more water to the channels or add a wet dish towel or sponge.*
>
> *If it is close to or above 65%, mop up some water, or tape some plastic wrap partway over the channels.*
>
> *Close the lid as quickly as you can, to prevent loss of humidity.*

Be sure to complete the following tasks at least 2–3 times every day (5 times is better), for Days 19–21 for standard chicken eggs (Days 16–21 for bantam chicken eggs):

Wash your hands.

Look and listen for signs of pipping and/or hatching, such as tiny cracks in the eggshell and/or a tapping noise.

Check the temperature inside the incubator without opening the lid. If it does not read 99.5 degrees F, adjust the temperature accordingly.

Check the humidity inside the incubator without opening the lid.

If it is close to or below 55% and there are no signs of hatching on any eggs: quickly open the lid and add more water to the channels, or add a wet dish towel or sponge. If it is close to or above 65%, mop up some water or tape some plastic wrap partway over the channels. Close the lid as quickly as you can, to prevent loss of humidity.

If it is close to or below 55% and there are signs of hatching on any eggs: DO NOT open the lid! There's too big a risk that a sudden drop in humidity could trap the chicks in their eggs.

DO NOT OPEN THE INCUBATOR UNLESS NECESSARY.
DO NOT TURN THE EGGS.

Blackbird Farm

Saturday, August 16

Mariposa García González

Heaven, where people help each other

Querida Abuelita,

We had the work-party picnic today, and it went pretty well!

Lupe and I met Sam and Chris at Redwood Farm this morning and got everything ready: task lists, tables for food, blankets on the grass, and lots and lots of sandwiches, with big mesh domes over them, so the flies and wasps couldn't land on the food.

Then everyone arrived, all at once. So many people came to help!

A tall Asian guy in a Superman T-shirt told me he was Gregory's friend George. He wanted to know if it was okay if he started fixing the chicken runs. He had a toolbox, and a tape measure clipped to his belt, so I figured he knew what he was doing. "Sure," I said.

Sam showed him where to start. (I think Sam's superpower is getting everybody organized.) Pretty soon I could hear hammering.

Gregory came too. It was weird to see him in jeans

and a Queen Latifah T-shirt instead of his mailman uniform. But you know what? He didn't look sad when he saw Agnes's farm this time. He looked ready to work. Sam told him that he was in charge of making sure at least one of the chicken coops got totally fixed up and made raccoon-proof by the end of the day, and he said he could do that. He put a big bowl of red beans and rice with a spoon sticking out of it on a not-too-rickety table, and headed off toward the sound of sawing.

Mom and Dad came next.

"So that's what those ladders are for," Dad said, staring at the weird ladders set up near the apple trees.

"Haven't you ever picked apples before?" I asked him.

He shook his head. "I only ever visited Uncle Jim earlier in the summer," he said. "The apples around here weren't ripe then, and he was too busy with the grapes for me to come later. I think I'll get my chance today, though."

"There are probably buckets in the barn, if you want to bring some out," I told him. "Maybe if you pick enough, we could make some apple crisp."

Then Ms. O'Malley wanted to know where she could put her gardening cake. (It had crunched-up Oreos on top, to look like dirt, and Gummy Worms sticking out of it; my chickens would have been impressed!) Her nephew came too—he's a white guy a little older than Lupe, maybe my cousin Javier's age. He was wearing a

Gravenstein Pizza T-shirt and jeans, and his sneakers had cool skulls on them. He brought a huge stack of pizzas in boxes, and even huger stacks of paper plates and napkins, which I hadn't even thought about. He took one look at the tables and asked Chris to come help him get some more tables out of his dad's catering van.

"It's a pleasure to be back at Redwood Farm," Ms. O'Malley told me. "I only wish Agnes could be here too." She put her cake on a table and started cutting it into pieces.

I nodded. But I couldn't help thinking that if Agnes was still alive, maybe I never would have gotten to visit Redwood Farm.

The extra tables really were helpful. I helped Ms. O'Malley's nephew set them all up in an L shape outside the blankets. There was a huge long one for drinks and a big bowl of ice, and another one for all the pizza, both with fancy paper tablecloths on them. (Sam stuck them on with tape.)

When we were done, I nodded at Ms. O'Malley's nephew. "Thanks," I told him. "This was really nice of you."

He smiled at me, kind of shy. "Thanks for inviting me," he said. "My favorite 4-H chickens were from Redwood Farm Supply. I'll never forget them. It's nice to be able to help out here."

I was pretty busy all afternoon. People had lots of

questions, and I didn't know all the answers, but since everyone was eating pizza and sandwiches and beans and rice and cake, they seemed okay waiting while we figured it out. Gregory stacked up huge piles of blackberry vines. His friend Mark brought his goats, so they started eating the leaves off right away. (I even got to hold their leashes while Mom took a picture!! Goats are great.)

George and Jane fixed all the loose wire fencing on the chicken coops. Chris's mom and her friend weeded Agnes's flower garden. Nobody fell off a ladder or out of an apple tree, and everyone seemed happy to take apples home, even the ones with icky bits you have to cut out. Farm people don't freak out because a bug chewed on their apples. Ms. O'Malley shared copies of her favorite applesauce recipe, and Sam's dad told everyone how to make apple crisp. (It's almost the same recipe as blackberry crisp, only with apples instead of blackberries. You squeeze a little lemon juice over the cut apples so they don't get brown, and you can skip the cornstarch.)

Chris found an old radio in Agnes's barn and replaced the batteries, and Lupe found a radio station with music that was good for getting work done. Dad came down off the ladder and taught Chris and Sam and Lupe how to do the Funky Chicken. (I helped, because I already know how.) Then Mom and Jane and Violet and Gregory and George taught everyone how to do the Macarena. (Ms. O'Malley really Macarena'd!) By this time, no one was working that hard, but not even Sam was upset, because most of the work was already done. So when Lupe started a dance-off, everyone joined in. No one agreed who won at the end, but it seemed like everyone had a really good time.

When we were driving home with the car full of bags of leftover apples (Dad wants to try making applesauce, and I guess I'd better make some apple crisp), Lupe didn't say, "I told you so." Instead, she just grinned at me and said, "Living on a farm is so much fun!"

"Thanks," I told her. "You were right. It was fun—for everyone, not just for me."

Maybe that is one of Lupe's superpowers: figuring out how everyone can have fun.

Te quiero,

Soficita

PS Sam found Agnes's Redwood Farm stamp in the barn. Lupe says of course I can use it; it's my farm, after all. There might not be chickens there yet, but it's almost ready for them now.

Sunday, August 17

Dear Gregory,

Thank you so much for coming to my work-party picnic. As you know, farming is hard work, and I have to make time for school and everything too, but I will try to keep everything in good shape from now on. It would have taken me weeks to get all that done by myself, so I really appreciate your help.

I hope you had a lot of fun too.

Your friend,
Sophie

PS Dad wants to know if you would give him your recipe for red beans and rice, because he'd like to make it for dinner tomorrow. He was sad everyone else ate it all before he could have any.

PPS Please tell George thanks too. Sorry, I don't know where to send his thank-you.

Sunday, August 17

Dear Ms. O'Malley's Nephew,

Please tell your dad thank you very much for the pizza
and the tables and the plates and the napkins and the
ice. They made things like a real party.

And thank you for coming to my work-party picnic
and helping out. It's a big relief to have a coop fixed up
and ready for my new chicks. Chickens are a lot of work,
but they're worth it. I guess you know that too.

I hope it was fun for you to see Redwood Farm, even
without Agnes's chickens there.

Your fellow chicken person,
Sophie

PS I'm sorry I didn't find out what your name is.

PPS What kind of chickens did you get from Redwood
Farm? Do you still have any of them? Do you know if
anyone else does? (Besides Ms. Griegson's Rhode Island
Reds.) I would really like to hear all about them, if you
have time someday.

Blackbird Farm

Monday, August 18

Mariposa Sofía García González
Heaven

Querida Abuelita,

Today was the first day of middle school. Mom and I
couldn't go back-to-school shopping this year, but Lupe
let me borrow a yellow T-shirt that was the perfect
color for me, and we covered one of Great-Uncle Jim's
old binders with pictures from feedstore catalogs and
stickers from Lupe's enormous sticker collection. Now,
instead of a beat-up old binder, it's a work of art.

It was the first day of Lupe's college too. Neither of
us ate very much for breakfast. Since Lupe's first class
started later than mine, she gave me a ride to school.

"Buena suerte, primita," she told me as I got my
backpack out of her car.

"You too, prima favorita," I told her. (I don't really
have a favorite cousin, but she looked nervous, and it
made her laugh.)

Then she drove off, and I went to find my homeroom:
world history.

When I got there, I was the only brown kid in class,

and all the white kids were already talking to each other, just like I thought. It felt like everybody was looking at me, but nobody said hi.

But then the door opened, and another brown girl came in, with straight black hair in two braids. She stood there for a minute, but no one said hi to her either. I may be shy, but I didn't want her to feel as lonely as I did. So I gave her a little wave.

She smiled at me and came over. "¿Hablas español?" she asked me.

"Sí," I told her. I wasn't the only girl at my new school who spoke Spanish after all!

A white guy who was older than my dad walked up to the front of the class. "I'm your teacher, Mr. Kivi," he told us. "This year we'll be learning world history, starting with the history of our families and where they came from. Today, I'd like each of you to tell me your full name, where your name comes from, and what your name means, if you know it."

The girl with the braids was frowning a little, like she was concentrating. Maybe she didn't speak that much English yet? "Decimos nuestros nombres, de dónde han venido y que significan," I told her very quietly in Spanish.

Mr. Kivi noticed. Oh, great, I thought. I'm going to be in trouble for talking in class in my very first five minutes of middle school.

But he didn't yell at me for talking in class. He stopped, and he asked, "¿Alguien quiere que hable español?" Not like he was calling me out for talking, or even asking us specifically. Just like he wondered if anyone needed a pencil.

I looked at the other new girl. She didn't look at me, just shook her head no. She didn't want him to speak Spanish.

I shook my head too. My face felt hot. People always assume I can't speak English, and I don't like it. I wished I hadn't done that to her.

Mr. Kivi waited a minute and then nodded. "I will start. My full name is written like this." And he wrote "Culhwch Ercwlff Kivi" on the board. "Does anyone want to try pronouncing it?"

The girl with the braids raised her hand. "Coolhuhweech Ehrkwolf Keevee," she sounded out.

"Very good effort!" he told her. "Here is how I pronounce it: Calwhook Ehrkvuf Keevee. I was teased in school for my name, so you should know I will absolutely not tolerate any jokes about names in my class—about my name or anyone else's!" He smiled, but I could tell he wasn't kidding. "Culhwch was one of King Arthur's cousins, and Culhwch and Ercwlff are Welsh names, from my mother's family. Most of my friends and family call me Cal. Kivi is a Finnish name, from my father's family. It means 'stone.'"

He nodded at the blond girl in the first desk. "Now, you," he told her.

"My name is Clara Marie Evans," she told him. "My mom thought the name Clara was pretty. They don't mean anything—they're just regular names."

"Are you certain?" Mr. Kivi asked Clara. "I have a dictionary of names and their meanings and origins here," he told us. "You can come in at lunch to find out what your name means, or you can do research at the library or on your own after school—try interviewing your family! I expect you to turn in one page on what you've learned, as homework."

Clara looked kind of annoyed, but maybe a little intrigued too.

Some kids knew where their names came from, and some didn't. One kid, whose middle name was Jehosephat, tried to make a joke about it, but Mr. Kivi shook his head and stopped him. "No teasing about names means not even your own name," he told the kid, whose first name was Aaron. "Names are important, and they deserve respect." Aaron nodded, but he didn't try to explain where Jehosephat was from or what it meant.

I know about my names, but I still hate talking in front of the class. I did okay, though. "My name is Sophia Mariposa Brown. My friends call me Sophie. Sophia means 'wisdom' and it was both of my grandmothers' middle names, even though one of them was from Mexico and one was from Wisconsin, so they spelled it differently. Mariposa was my mother's mother's first name, and Brown is my father's last name. If I was born in Mexico, my name might have been Sophia Mariposa Brown González, because lots of people have two last names there. But mine is just Brown."

We kept going around the room while I recovered and let my breathing slow down again. Then we got to the girl next to me.

"My name is Xochitl Ximena Ramirez. Xochitl means 'flower.' It comes from Mexico, like me. My family is from Mexico and from El Salvador." She looked around the class and smiled. "You can call me Xochi."

After we got our textbooks and heard more about what we'd be studying, a bell rang, and we had to go to different classrooms for our next class.

"Sorry about that," I told Xochi.

She shrugged. "I speak English, too."

"See you at lunch?" I asked. Everyone has lunch at the same time.

She shrugged again. Then she grabbed her books and hurried off into the hall.

I had math class next. When I got my first schedule, the school put me in math for people who need more help. I don't know why, because I'm really good at math, and I've always gotten A's in it before. But Mom went in and explained to the school that they made a mistake and needed to fix it, so now I'm in harder math.

I flipped through my textbook. It didn't look too hard.

But I don't know anyone in the class, and we only talked about math.

Then it was lunch. "I met this girl in my homeroom, called Xochi," I told Sam and Chris, looking around for Xochi when we came into the cafeteria. I didn't see her, though.

I finished my egg-salad sandwich while Sam and Chris tried to sing the song they learned in Spanish class.

"Dos arbol-ritos que something something eh-else," Sam sang, batting her eyes like butterflies at Chris. They both giggled.

I tried not to get annoyed. "Your teacher should play some Bomba Estéreo or Ana Tijoux or something people our age actually listen to," I told them. But they just kept laughing and messing around until I told them to quit it. I didn't like them making fun of Spanish, even if it was a silly song.

I have PE with Sam, and the teacher let us pick whether to drill with soccer balls or play soccer. Sam isn't exactly great at soccer, so we drilled together until PE was over. I think she's getting a little better. She just hasn't practiced that much.

They only teach beginning Spanish here, and I already know Spanish, so I had study hall in the library next instead of language class.

So does Xochi. I still felt bad about my mistake this

morning. But I didn't want that to stop us from maybe
being friends. So I gathered up my nerve, and I asked her
if I could sit at her table. And she said yes!

After that, we talked about everything. I told her
how I moved to a farm from LA, and how my mom writes
articles and my dad is trying to learn to farm, and how
I have chickens now, and eggs that will hatch, and how
Lupe came to live with us for a while.

Xochi told me about some of the places she lived,
when her family was moving from farm to farm,
following where the work was. Now her dad is Mr.
Moreno's new ranch manager, so they don't have to move
anymore, and her abuela came to live with them too.

I wish you lived with us. I bet you would have
loved it.

Then the teacher-librarian told us we might want to
get some homework done while we had the chance, so
I worked on my world history homework and read Part
Two of my hatching instructions.

Finding my bus home wasn't complicated at all. I
guess that's one good thing about small schools.

After I checked on my eggs, I read to my chickens.
They're not very quiet, but it's hard to worry too much
about school while they're buk-buk-bukking around
the barnyard, closing their eyes in the sun and fluffing
up their feathers, and rolling around in the dust. My
chickens are always glad to see me.

At dinner, Lupe and I both shared about our days. College sounds really hard, but Lupe likes it so far.

Mom was pretty excited about my name assignment. She told me about her name, and she said it gave her all kinds of ideas for articles. (I think Mom's superpower is that she can turn almost anything into an article and earn money writing it.) When I asked Dad about his name, it turns out he didn't know much about it. I told him about the name dictionaries, and he said maybe it was time he learned something about his own name. I told him I'd help.

Te extraño,
Soficita

PS After dinner, I told each of my chickens about their names, and how they got them. After all, names are important.

Monday, August 18
Mr. Kivi—World History
Family history project
Part One: Names

The name that I say first is: <u>Sophia</u>

Meaning: <u>Wisdom</u>

Origin: <u>Greek (which is weird, because I'm not Greek and neither were my grandmothers)</u>

My middle name(s) is/are: <u>Mariposa</u>

Meaning(s): <u>Butterfly</u>

Origin: <u>Spanish (it was my abuela's first name)</u>

The name(s) I say last is/are: <u>Brown</u>

Meaning(s): <u>brown, you know, like the color</u>

Origin: <u>English, Irish, and Scottish, but my dad thinks ours is Scottish</u>

Something I love about my name: <u>That it's beautiful and it all comes from my family.</u>

Something I wish was different about my name: <u>I wish people would stop saying I don't look like a Sophie. Maybe they don't know any other Sophies who look like me, but that doesn't mean it's not my name. Also, I don't like it when people laugh when I tell them my last name is Brown. Yeah, I'm brown. So??</u>

Blackbird Farm

Tuesday, August 19

Mariposa García González
Heaven

Querida Abuelita,

Before we moved here, I knew middle school was going to keep me busy. I just didn't know I'd be taking care of a flock of unusual chickens and incubating a bunch of eggs too. Now every morning I have to turn the eggs and feed the chickens and give them clean water, and every afternoon I have to check the eggs and do my homework and work on my chicken observations and make sure my chickens are still okay. But all the farmers I know are busy people too, so I guess it's good practice.

Going to school here isn't like it was in LA, but I'm doing okay, so far. English will be fine, since I already know how to do punctuation and grammar, and some of the books look good.

Biology might be fun. I wish I knew someone in class, though. When Ms. Low (aka Violet's friend Cindy) asked us to tell her one thing we hope to learn about this year, I told her I wanted to learn about hatching poultry, and everyone laughed, not in a nice way. She told me later that the kids here already learned that in second grade. But she also told me we'd have individual projects to work on, and that just because they'd learned about eggs didn't mean kids here had necessarily hatched their own chicks.

Tech class is cool. I already have some ideas for my first project. I never knew I could learn to code and make games and stuff. I thought that was something you only learned in college or at a computer job. Maybe when I grow up I'll be a coder and a poultry farmer.

The arts teacher figured out right away that singing in tune isn't my strong point, though. He was really surprised, since he says I'm from such a musical culture. Maybe he doesn't know that not all Latinas sing like J.Lo? (He should hear Mom sing—you know she's worse than I am!) He's trying me on finger cymbals instead. I like the finger cymbals, but I don't like being the only one with them. He kept saying that I just need to Listen to the Music and Sing What I Hear! If I could do that, singing would be my strong point, wouldn't it? But there's only a few more weeks of music, and then it's dance and watercolor and theater and maybe ceramics, if they can find someone who can fix the kiln in time.

Today I saw Xochi at lunch. She waved at me, and I went over to join her. When Chris and Sam came in,

I waved at them—but they didn't come over and sit with us. They went and sat together by themselves. What's that about?

I was so happy to make friends here. I forgot that sometimes friends are kind of complicated too.

At least Lupe is having a good week. Well, except for statistics. Today she came home in tears, and after some hugs and tissues and talking to Mom for a while, she's decided she's going to take statistics next quarter, and instead she's going to switch to a business class, with some math but also some business stuff.

But, other than that, college is going really well for her. She says it's not too hard, and no one else has yelled anything mean, and that when I'm ready I can totally do it, even statistics. She found the college's Latinx Student Union club that Violet told her about too. They're having a party this weekend, and she's going. When Mom asked her with who, Lupe smiled and didn't really answer. And she talked for almost an hour on the phone to a girl she met called Yoon, who wants to be a teacher too. I think they're going to do a project together. (Although mostly they talked about Yoon's roller-derby league, which sounds awesome, but probably isn't for college.)

I know just what you'd say if you were here: "My goodness, Soficita, ¡cómo has crecido!" And you'd be right: I really have grown, inside and out. After all, I'm in middle school now.

Te extraño mucho,
Soficita

PS It's really hard to keep the humidity in my incubator right. I have to add more water almost every day, but when I open the lid to add the water, the humidity gets even lower. I hope my eggs will be okay.

CHICKEN AWARD

THIS CHICKEN AWARD IS PRESENTED TO

CHAMELEON

FOR HER GOLD MEDAL DUST-BATHING
PERFORMANCE. EXTRA POINTS FOR CREATIVITY
WHEN SHE MADE HERSELF LOOK LIKE A GIANT LUMP
OF WIGGLING DUST.

Sophia Mariposa Brown

Sophia Mariposa Brown, unusual poultry farmer
Tuesday, August 19

Blackbird Farm

Wednesday, August 20

Mariposa García González

Heaven

Querida Abuelita,

Xochi waits for me at the lunchroom door now, and then
we go find Sam and Chris. I wish they all were friends
with each other the way they are with me. But you can't
make people be friends. I talked to Lupe about it the
other day, and she said sometimes people make friends
right away, and sometimes it takes longer. Sometimes old
friends get jealous of new friends, like when Aquí and Allí
came to live with my chickens. And sometimes people
aren't used to being friends with someone whose life was
kind of different from theirs. But Lupe also reminded me
that I don't have to give up being friends with anyone to
make someone else happy. Anyone who tells me who I can
and can't be friends with isn't a real friend.

I don't have a lot of friends here, so I'm glad they're
all real friends so far.

I'm glad I have study hall with Xochi. We get so
much homework done! Some days Xochi says she wants
to speak English, but other times she wants a break, so
we speak Spanish. I told her my dad says Spanish still

130

makes his brain tired, even though he's pretty fluent, because he didn't grow up speaking it, like me and Mom, and he still has to think about what the words mean all the time. But, he says it's absolutely worth all that work.

It's nice to spend some time just with Xochi. We have things in common that Chris and Sam don't always understand. Like cousins that are almost like siblings, and that frutas con chile y limón are great and not gross. (Xochi likes watermelon best; I can't decide whether orange or pineapple is my favorite.) It's not like I'd hang out with her if she was mean, just because she's Xicana too. But she isn't mean—she's really nice, and I like having a friend to share that stuff with again.

I bet you'd like her, and Chris and Sam too. I wish you could meet them.

Te extraño,
Soficita

PS I think Xochi's superpower is that she's really brave. If she has a question, she just raises her hand and asks it, in front of everyone. Today she asked the teacher-librarian if we could kick a fútbol on the grass in front of the library. And the teacher-librarian said sure! I'm so glad she's my friend now too.

PPS I told Xochi about my chickens' superpowers. She can't wait to meet them!

Blackbird Farm

Agnes Taylor
Unearthly Poultry Farm

Dear Agnes,

When you were alive, did your brain ever get tired from learning a lot of new things at once? Mine did this week. Maybe it's a good thing my middle school is small, since I had to learn everyone's names, and where all my classes were, and remember to do all my homework as well as all my chicken chores and egg chores. But it's the weekend now, and Lupe says next week will be way easier, now that we know what we're doing.

You know what isn't easy? Trying to guess how much to turn the temperature dial on your incubator. It would be a lot easier if it had a dial like an oven, where you tell it what temperature you want it to be, instead of only "Increase" and "Decrease." This morning it was cold out. I read the thermometer inside the incubator through the window in the lid, and it said 98.5 degrees F. I kind of panicked, and turned the dial toward "Increase." Nothing happened, but it never really does right away—it takes hours to heat up and cool down.

I checked it as soon as I got home from school, and

it said it was 100.5 degrees F in there! So I turned it to "Decrease," just a tiny, tiny bit. Now it's cooled off outside, and my incubator thermometer says 98.5 degrees F again. Argh!

Maybe I'll never hatch enough chickens to fill all your coops back up.

I'm sorry. I'm trying really hard to get it right.

Your friend,
Sophie

Agnes Taylor

Your version of heaven

Dear Agnes,

Today Chris and Sam and Xochi came over after school
so we could work on our science projects. Middle school
is a lot of work, but it isn't so bad when you can read your
library books and take notes and hang out with your
chickens and your friends on a beautiful not-too-hot day,
while you eat leftover apple crisp.

Sam is researching why llamas spit, how it works
(biologically speaking), and what to do if you get llama
spit on you. (Llama spit isn't really just spit—it's more
like projectile vomit, Sam says. It sounds SO GROSS!
I hope I get to see Ella do it someday. Sam says you
shouldn't go around trying to make llamas spit, though,
because it upsets them and leaves a horrible taste in
their mouths.)

Chris is researching the different kinds of sounds
chickens make to communicate and learning how to
do them so well the chickens pay attention. (He could
already do the "Look out! There's a hawk!" noise, but

now he can do the "Treats! Excellent!!" noise too. We had to bring out some sunflower seeds from Agnes's barn so my chickens weren't so disappointed every time they rushed over to see what he'd found.) He's teaching me the sounds too, because after all, exceptional poultry farmers need to know everything they can learn about their chickens. Chris says just because you aren't born with any superpowers doesn't mean you can't learn how to do amazing things. Like Batman. Only, not rich. (I have to admit, talking to chickens is a pretty great superpower.)

Xochi is researching garrobos (a kind of iguana), where they live, what they eat, and how to take care of them. She wants to be a zookeeper when she grows up, so she learns about different kinds of animals every year. This year, it's iguanas and lizards and chameleons and Komodo dragons, so she figured she might as well get school credit for the stuff she wanted to learn about anyway.

And I'm researching chicken embryos and how they develop in eggs. I don't care that Clara said it was a little-kid project. I'm a poultry farmer, like you, and I'm hatching eggs from your chickens, so I need to know what's going on in there. My dad says he's never going to be too old to want to learn new things, and my mom says the stuff you learn is your greatest treasure, plus it's impossible to steal. I can't share my chicken-observation notes with the class, since Ms. Low doesn't know about unusual chickens. But I can share what I learn about regular chicken eggs.

After we worked on our science projects, Chris and Xochi and Sam helped me think up experiments we could do with my chickens. Not evil-scientist ones, of course—just stuff that would be good to know, like what are the heaviest things Henrietta can lift, and how fast Roadrunner can go. Xochi said zookeepers have to know all about their animals, to keep the animals and the people safe. I guess it's probably the same with unusual chickens.

I'll let you know what we learn.

Your friend,
Sophie

PS Tomorrow, I start Part Two of your checklist. Wish me luck.

PPS Xochi told me she asked her parents if she could have iguanas, or maybe chickens. And they said no iguanas, but maybe chickens! I think she'd be great with chickens.

THURSDAY, AUGUST 21

Chicken Embryo Stages
(Standard Chickens)

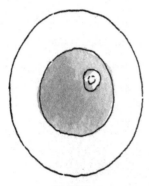

DAY 1:
Pretty much a blob

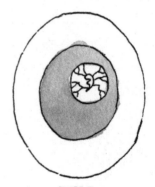

DAY 3:
Starts getting leg and wing bumps

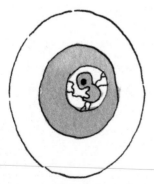

DAY 5:
Eyes developing

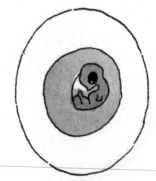

DAY 6:
Beak forming;
can move around

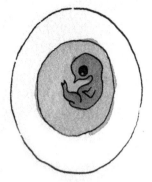

DAY 8:
Feet and wings growing

DAY 10:
Feathers forming;
beak hardening

DAY 14:
Claws developing

DAYS 12-16:
Getting into hatching position
(I hope you're ready in there, chicks!)

DAYS 19-20:
Absorbing yolk sac

DAY 21: Time to hatch!

CHICKEN AWARD

THIS CHICKEN AWARD IS PRESENTED TO

AQUÍ

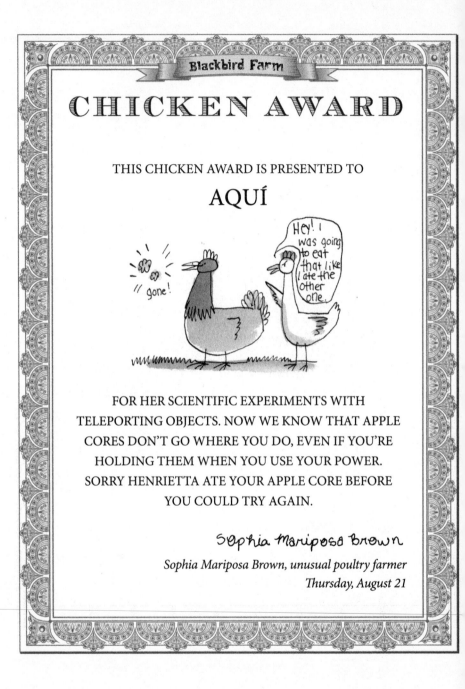

FOR HER SCIENTIFIC EXPERIMENTS WITH
TELEPORTING OBJECTS. NOW WE KNOW THAT APPLE
CORES DON'T GO WHERE YOU DO, EVEN IF YOU'RE
HOLDING THEM WHEN YOU USE YOUR POWER.
SORRY HENRIETTA ATE YOUR APPLE CORE BEFORE
YOU COULD TRY AGAIN.

Sophia Mariposa Brown

Sophia Mariposa Brown, unusual poultry farmer
Thursday, August 21

Blackbird Farm

Friday, August 22

Agnes Taylor

Heaven's Best Unusual Poultry Farm

Dear Agnes,

Did you know the farm you left me is kind of famous?

Lupe came home from college today all excited because when she told her business class about our work-party picnic, her professor recognized Redwood Farm and said she had a former student who had done a project on it. She said she'd get in touch with him and see if he'd like to come talk to us.

I'd like to talk to someone about what it was like when people used to order chickens and eggs from you, and when you had chickens living in all those coops. I have some questions, and I guess you can't answer them now.

Your friend,
Sophie

PS My eggs are supposed to hatch tomorrow. I really hope they're on time, because Mom is not going to let me stay home from school to take care of them.

Date: Saturday, August 23
To: Hortensia James <hjames@APeculiarKindofBird.com>
From: Sophie Brown <unusualchickenfarmer@gmail.com>
Subject: Eggs aren't hatching

Dear Hortensia,

Are you sure those eggs you sent me are really going to hatch? They were supposed to hatch today, so I've been waiting in the barn all day with them. What am I supposed to do if they don't hatch this weekend? Are the chicks going to starve or die of thirst or overheating if they hatch when I'm not there to move them out of the incubator?

    I'm sorry I don't already know all this stuff. I'm following Agnes's instructions, but they aren't always that clear. So I'm going to keep asking questions until I know what to do.

Sorry,
Sophie

PS If I did something wrong and they won't ever hatch, I'm really sorry. I tried my best.

Date: Saturday, August 23
To: Sophie Brown <unusualchickenfarmer@gmail.com>
From: Hortensia James <hjames@APeculiarKindofBird.com>
Subject: RE: Eggs aren't hatching

Dear Sophie,

Of course you should ask questions. How else will you learn everything you need to know to take care of unusual poultry?

Remember that these are chicks, not robots. They won't all hatch right on time, or even on the same day. And you shouldn't open the incubator until all the eggs have hatched in high humidity, and all the chicks have dried off in the nice, warm incubator. Do you know what humidity is? It's the amount of water in the air. You are monitoring yours, right?

You don't need to worry about the chicks starving or dying of thirst, even if they're in there for a couple of days. After all, they've just absorbed an egg yolk that's as big as they are! That's plenty of food. They're fine for up to 72 hours after hatching.

MOST IMPORTANT PART: Whatever happens, don't try to help chicks hatch. The chick's body is still adapting to its final, outside form, and if it comes out before it's ready, it could bleed to death. The chicks know what they're doing, even if they need to stop and take breaks occasionally. That's fine—they'll still hatch when they're ready—so let them get out of their shells by themselves. If you're really worried about one, ask a local poultry person to consult with you before you do anything.

Best of luck,
Hort

PS How old are you, Sophie?

PPS You do know some other poultry people, right?

Date: Saturday, August 23
To: Hortensia James <hjames@APeculiarKindofBird.com>
From: Sophie Brown <unusualchickenfarmer@gmail.com>
Subject: RE: RE: Eggs aren't hatching

Dear Hort,

Yes, I know what humidity is. If I didn't, I know how to look up a word, and then if I don't know the words in the definition, I look those words up too. I'm almost thirteen. I know how to use a dictionary. And yes, I'm monitoring my humidity.

But I didn't know the part about not helping the chicks, so thank you. I bet people who try to help and kill their chicks by accident feel awful. I know that waiting can be hard, but I can handle it.

Thank you for answering my questions,
Sophie

PS Yes, I know some poultry people who can help. I will call them if I need to. I just thought I'd ask you first, since they were your eggs. Sorry to bother you.

PPS I like your nickname. Thanks for telling it to me. I know that people who work together aren't always friends, but I still appreciate your help. Sophie is my usual nickname, or Soficita, but you can call me Soph if you want to.

Date: Saturday, August 23
To: Sophie Brown <unusualchickenfarmer@gmail.com>
From: Hortensia James <hjames@APeculiarKindofBird.com>
Subject: RE: RE: RE: Eggs aren't hatching

Dear Soph,

You can ask me whatever you need to. It's no bother. I'm glad you have people there who can see your eggs in person. Sometimes it's easier to tell what to do when you can see them for yourself. But I will still try to help you.

Your friend, I hope,
Hort

Date: Sunday, August 24
To: Hortensia James <hjames@APeculiarKindofBird.com>
From: Sophie Brown <unusualchickenfarmer@gmail.com>
Subject: Eggs ARE hatching!!!

Dear Hort,

One of the eggs has started to hatch!!! You were right. I just had to wait longer than I thought. The chick inside made a tiny hole in the shell by itself. Chris says it's called a pip, and it's so the chick can breathe. It's a good thing you already told me not to help them at all, or I might have wondered if I should help the rest make their air holes, so they don't suffocate in there. Now I know they'll do it on their own when they're ready. (I asked my friend Chris to come help me watch them and make sure I didn't help by accident. He is a poultry person and has raised his own chicks.)

I hope the chick finishes hatching soon, and the rest of them too. I don't want to miss it while I'm at school.

Your friend,
Soph

Blackbird Farm

Sunday, August 24

Agnes Taylor
Heavenly Hatchery

Dear Agnes,

Chris came over to hang out in the barn and help me
wait for my eggs to hatch. (Sam had to do llama chores,
and Xochi was doing errands with her grandmother.)
We waited and waited and waited and then one of them
started to pip. It was so weird to see this egg start
moving on its own!

We think it took a nap after it made a tiny hole,
because it didn't do anything for forever. But Chris just
kept telling me this was normal, and not to open the lid
to check on it, and not to help it. You'd have been proud
of Chris. He paid attention to all the instructions we had
and made sure I followed them.

We were quiet and listened hard, and we could hear
the chick peeping! It didn't sound like a chicken at all—
more like one of those little brown birds that lives in
bushes. A wild bird. It sounded kind of mad and kind of
sad, but I still didn't help it.

Then another chick started to pip! And it peeped

too! I wondered what they were telling each other. Were they doing "We can do it!" speeches, like before a soccer game? Or were they competing to see who could be the first out of the shell, like my little cousins would?

The first chick pipped all the way around the whole shell. It took forever! But we didn't help it. We saw the chick inside, but it didn't look like a chicken at all. It looked like it had long wet hair, like a bedraggled tiny fluffy dog that was going bald, so you could see the pink skin underneath. It wasn't gross and bloody or anything, though, just wet. (I didn't know what to expect, so I was kind of nervous about that.)

All of a sudden the egg fell over, and a wing stuck out. It was covered in wet fluff and shaped sort of like a triangle.

Then I guess it took another nap, while the other chick worked on pipping its shell and peeping at the top of its lungs. The second chick seemed mad that the first chick wasn't answering. Or maybe it liked peeping without anyone interrupting. Chris and I tried peeping back to it, and it took breaks to listen.

Then the first chick started flailing its wing around, and knocked itself over, and the shell started to break in half a little wider. And then we could see a beak! And an eye! After that, it kind of rolled out of its shell, and flailed around, and unfolded itself until I could see it had all its chicken parts, but like a tiny rubber chicken with a partly bald wig all over it.

Then it fell over, stopped peeping, and didn't move at all. I freaked out. I thought it had died. Chris told me no, chicks do this all the time. They just get really worn out from all this living, so they stop wherever they are and have naps.

Meanwhile, another chick had started pipping! Little bits of shell were getting everywhere, and all that loud peeping was kind of overwhelming too.

Chris calmed me down by going over the next steps. We are supposed to wait until the chicks are all done hatching, and until they are dried off. Then we can finally open the lid. I have a brooder box set up near the incubator in the barn, which is really just a cardboard box with a heat lamp hanging over it, and food and water and some wood shavings inside.

The chicks still weren't dry when Chris finally had to go home. Dad brought me some hand sanitizer and dinner in the barn, so I wouldn't have to leave the chicks to come in. Even though he's not really a chicken person, he thought the chicks hatching was pretty cool, so he went and got Mom and Lupe. We all stood around and ate sandwiches and listened to the chicks peeping. Mom asked me lots of questions in case she ever needs to write an article on hatching chicks.

I don't know whether I hope they're all done by the

time I wake up tomorrow, so I can see them before I go to school, or whether I hope they aren't, so maybe I can watch more of them come out of their shells. Whatever they want, I guess. It's their birthdays, after all.

Your friend,
Soph

Blackbird Farm

Monday, August 25

Agnes Taylor

Up There Watching Over Unusual Chicks (I hope)

Dear Agnes,

I woke up extra early this morning so I could check on the chicks as well as my chickens before school. It's not that easy, being a poultry farmer and having to go to school too. Were you a poultry farmer when you were a kid? Or did you wait until you were done with school?

The humidity and temperature were still okay, thank goodness. All the chicks that had started hatching were out of their shells now. A couple of them were flopped over, looking dead. One of them was on top of another egg, and another had its head still curled up in an eggshell. But the other two were moving around, peeping. They were starting to dry off, and I could see that they were kind of dark brownish gray, with yellow heads. But they weren't all dry yet, and not all of them had hatched, so I left them in there and didn't open the lid at all. I'll hurry home right after school and see how they're doing.

Your friend,
Soph

Date: Monday, August 25
To: Hortensia James <hjames@APeculiarKindofBird.com>
From: Sophie Brown <unusualchickenfarmer@gmail.com>
Subject: These eggs aren't hatching, though

Dear Hort,

Four chicks have hatched. They're still in the incubator. I think they're doing okay.

But what about the other eggs that haven't done anything yet?

Your friend,
Soph

Dear Hort,

Gregory came by to deliver our mail. He's a poultry person too, and he's my 4-H leader, so I asked him about my eggs, since you haven't emailed me back yet. He showed me how to do a thing called candling, where you shine a flashlight through your eggs. Lupe turned the barn light off so we could see, and Gregory held his hand around the flashlight with an egg on top, so the light shined through it, and I had my hands ready to catch the egg, in case it rolled off or started to hatch or something. Two of them just looked yellow, so we think those might not have grown chicks. One of them looks mostly dark, so we think there's a chick inside that one. But when will it come out? Is it stuck in there??

Please email me back,
Soph

PS Sorry I didn't know about candling before. I'm learning as fast as I can.

Dear Soph,

Sometimes it's hard for me to check my email when I'm out working on my own farm, but I'll always respond when I can. Good work learning to candle your eggs—that's just what I would have suggested. Please give Gregory my thanks for showing you how. In the future, you can candle new eggs before you put them into the incubator. With practice, you'll learn to see which ones have embryos developing inside and which ones don't. It's best to keep any that aren't developing out of the incubator. But since we're not entirely sure with these, you can keep them in for now.

By my calculations, you're now at Day 20. Bantam eggs usually hatch by now, but it's not uncommon for chicks to hatch late—keep remembering, chicks are not robots. They have their own schedules.

If there's any pipping from the unhatched eggs, or you hear peeping from them, leave the hatched chicks in the incubator a little longer. You want the incubator to be at the proper humidity when the other eggs hatch, and it won't be if you open the lid.

If there's no pipping or peeping from the unhatched eggs, you can quickly and carefully move the hatched chicks to your brooder box (you have that set up, right?) when they're all dried off.

Either way, leave the unhatched eggs alone and wait

patiently until tomorrow, Day 21. If they still haven't pipped or peeped at Day 21, email me and I'll tell you what to do.

Best of luck,
Hort

PS Sometimes I wish I didn't have to be so patient to be a good poultry farmer. Don't you?

Date: Tuesday, August 26
To: Hortensia James <hjames@APeculiarKindofBird.com>
From: Sophie Brown <unusualchickenfarmer@gmail.com>
Subject: Some eggs still aren't hatching

Dear Hort,

It's the morning of Day 21, and I still have three eggs that aren't doing anything at all in the incubator. So I'm emailing you like you said to.

Your fellow patient poultry farmer,
Soph

PS I moved the dried-off chicks to the brooder box, so there's nothing in the incubator except for the eggs.

PPS It's making me really sad just to look at those eggs. I hope the chicks aren't dead in there.

Date: Tuesday, August 26
To: Sophie Brown <unusualchickenfarmer@gmail.com>
From: Hortensia James <hjames@APeculiarKindofBird.com>
Subject: RE: Some eggs still aren't hatching

Dear Soph,

I know just what you mean. I've spent so many years becoming the best poultry farmer I can be, and I still feel like I've failed every time one of my eggs doesn't hatch. But the truth is, some eggs just don't work out, and it can be hard to know exactly what's going on in there. It's time to test these ones and see if you need to wait a little longer, or move on and take care of the ones that are in the world.

Here's what to do now. It's called the float test, and it's the best test we have for this sort of situation.

1. Find a big bowl—big enough for your three eggs to fit on the bottom without stacking on top of each other. Glass is easier, so you can look into it from the side instead of just the top and see exactly what's happening, but any kind that holds water will work.
2. Fill partway with warm water (100 degrees F) so it's full enough to cover the eggs once you put them in, but not so full it will overflow.
3. Listen and look carefully one more time to make sure there's no pipping or peeping from the unhatched eggs. If there is, don't open the incubator lid!
4. If there isn't, carefully open the lid and take an egg

out. Gently lower it into the water as carefully as possible. Repeat with the other eggs.

5. Wait until the water stops moving. Watch the eggs to see which of these apply:

A) The egg sinks to the bottom and stays there. No chick ever grew in this egg, and it isn't ever going to hatch. Keep it out of the incubator so it doesn't go bad and explode, contaminating the others.

B) The egg floats to the top and about half or more of it sticks out of the water. This embryo didn't make it and won't hatch. Keep it out of the incubator too.

C) The egg floats with only a little bit sticking out. It might stay still, or it might move around. This egg still needs time to hatch; carefully fish it out and put it back in the incubator!

Best of luck,
Hort

PS Let me know what you learn.

Date: Tuesday, August 26
To: Hortensia James <hjames@APeculiarKindofBird.com>
From: Sophie Brown <unusualchickenfarmer@gmail.com>
Subject: RE: RE: Some eggs still aren't hatching

Dear Hort,

After school today, I did the float test exactly like you told me to. Thank you for the help.

I listened very, very carefully. My friends Chris and Sam listened too, in case their ears were better. None of us heard anything, none of the eggs were moving at all, and we couldn't see any cracks, not even tiny ones.

So I did it: I opened the lid. I took out the eggs, very, very carefully. I put them in a bowl with the warm water. (Yes, we measured the temperature first. Those old thermometers are really hard to read, but luckily Chris has had practice with them.)

Two of the eggs went straight to the bottom and stayed there, without moving at all.

But one of them went down a little and then started floating up.

Chris started telling it not to be a dead floater. Sam covered her eyes. I held my breath.

We watched as the egg floated up to the surface—but only a little bit of it stuck out of the water. Slowly, the water grew still.

And then—then the egg wiggled.

I never knew an egg could do that before the chick wanted out! Chris yelled that it was a good egg—no, a great egg, and a fighter, and it was going to make it! Sam uncovered her eyes. We watched it wiggle a couple more times. Then I got scared that maybe it was going to start pipping right there and drown, so I very carefully fished it out and put it back in the incubator and closed the lid.

I didn't feel right just throwing the other two eggs away, even though they sank. So Chris and Sam and I buried them back by the henhouse. Sam dug a deep hole, and Chris found some broken-up concrete chunks in one of Great-Uncle Jim's junk piles to put over them so nothing would dig them up. I put the eggs carefully in the hole and said a few goodbye words, even though I know you said they hadn't even started to develop, so really no one was in there. Then we covered them all up and went in to see if the egg that wiggled was doing anything.

We're still waiting.

Your friend,
Soph

PS My friend Xochitl says thank you for sharing the float test with us. She's going to be a zookeeper, so she was very happy to learn about it. She's going to help me with it next time, if she can. She wants to know if it works for reptiles too. And what about platypuses?

Date: Tuesday, August 26
To: Hortensia James <hjames@APeculiarKindofBird.com>
From: Sophie Brown <unusualchickenfarmer@gmail.com>
Subject: Chick hatched!!!

Dear Hort,

The last chick hatched!!! When it dries off, I'll put it in with the others.

Thank you,
Soph

PS Are the other chicks going to be mean to it, since it's new to the flock? Or is that just a grown-up-chicken thing?

Date: Wednesday, August 27
To: Sophie Brown <unusualchickenfarmer@gmail.com>
From: Hortensia James <hjames@APeculiarKindofBird.com>
Subject: RE: Chick hatched!!!

Dear Soph,

Congratulations on a very successful hatch!

You should be able to add the last chick to your flock in the brooder box without any pecking-order issues. These chicks are too young to be sorting out who's the boss yet. They're busy just eating, drinking, sleeping, and pooping. That was a good thing to check on, though.

For the next three to five weeks, you'll have your hands full taking care of all of them, I'm sure. It's amazing how much dust and mess a few little fluffy chicks can cause!

You might want to start thinking about adding roosts to your brooder box, so they can start practicing sitting on them in a few days. Keep in mind that their feet will still be very small, so they can't hold on to big branches, but they're heavy enough by then that a tiny twig won't work either.

I'd love to see a picture, if you have time to take one! I never get tired of seeing those adorable fluffy little creatures.

Your friend,
Hort

PS I'm sure you already know this, but do not under any circumstances put your new chicks in with your adult chickens. Most chickens don't know enough to be nice to baby chicks they didn't hatch.

PPS I'm afraid I don't know a thing about reptiles or platypuses. Sorry.

Date: Thursday, August 28
To: Hortensia James <hjames@APeculiarKindofBird.com>
From: Sophie Brown <unusualchickenfarmer@gmail.com>
Subject: RE: RE: Chick hatched!!!

Dear Hort,

Here is a picture that we took on Lupe's phone. This was the cutest one. Sorry my thumb got in the way a little bit.

You know, those chicks really do make huge messes! I see now why you sent me that other waterer that hangs. Every time I fill up the one that's like a dish, one of the chicks jumps in it or falls in it or walks in it and gets the water all over the shavings, and then they all try to sit in the wet shavings. I guess the chicks just don't have very much sense yet. I worry that they'll get cold and sick and die, so now I'm just using your waterer.

There is one chick that has a little more sense, though, maybe. I haven't named any of them yet, because I don't really know who they are yet. But this is the chick that hatched the last, the one whose egg floated, and it's light gray, like smoke, with a yellow head. When everyone else is rushing for the wet shavings, this one always stays warm and dry in the corner. Chris says we should name it Gandalf, because Gandalf was a wise wizard who was known as Gandalf the Grey in some books and movies. But I'm not sure it would be a good idea to name a chicken after a wizard. Especially not one of mine.

We'll see.

Your friend,
Soph

PS I figured it would be a bad idea to put the chicks in with my chickens. But I hope they can meet them someday, when they're older.

Agnes Taylor
Heavenly Roost

Dear Agnes,

I'm sorry to say that someone left trash in your front yard. Or maybe the wind blew it there, or a whole bunch of crows brought it there, or something. Lupe and I cleaned it up, but it made me sad that someone would treat your farm like that.

Lupe squeezed my shoulder. "It's just because people think no one is living here, so it doesn't matter."

But people here knew you, and they know it's my farm now. Maybe they think it doesn't matter to me. Or maybe they don't like that Redwood Farm is mine now.

Anyway, that's not why we were there. We went to see what we could use to build a practice roost for my new chicks. I never knew this before, but Lupe took shop class in high school and knows how to use a bunch of Great-Uncle Jim's tools! So she is going to help me build them something great, and then I will learn how to use the tools too.

Thanks to all those people helping out at our work-party picnic, I think the chicken coops are ready to go! We checked very carefully, and all the wire mesh is stuck tight to the wood frames, with no loose parts or gaps, and the doors latch shut, and there aren't any plants growing inside that could be poisonous to chickens. (There are a few blackberry vines trying to come in again already, but I know those aren't poisonous to chickens because my chickens peck the leaves off of them all the time.)

There are eight empty coops right now. They made me sad, because what's the point of a coop without any chickens in it? But I've already got chicks getting ready to go into the first coop, and more eggs will be coming soon. I'm pretty excited to fill every one of them with chickens again. I mean, it will be a lot of work, but most kids around here have chores and things they have to do. I bet it won't be nearly as much work as Sam's llama, or even Chris's mom's vegetable garden. (It's ENORMOUS! You could park more than ten cars in her garden, I bet.)

We found some wood in the barn to build a stand for your chick roosts. Lupe says we can build something where we can change out the size of the roost as the chicks' feet get bigger. I'm really excited! I've never exactly built anything before, only helped Dad try to put the Ikea furniture together. (I'm better at paying attention to the details in the pictures than he is. I only put something together upside down once. But he's better at checking to make sure we have all the parts and tools ready than I am. We're a good team.)

After we cleaned the dust and cobwebs off of our supplies and put them in the car, we went to Jane's feedstore to watch the chicks there. I wanted to see if mine looked like any of the breeds she has. Some did, but they were all different breeds. Chicks don't look very much like the adult chickens they grow up to be. We spent a while watching the chicks wander around and fall asleep on each other. Lupe could not get over how cute they were.

I asked Jane if she had any locks we could put on your coop doors.

Jane looked concerned. "Are you having problems with chicken thieves again?"

"Wait—what?" Lupe said. I guess I never told her about what happened before.

I shook my head. "No—not yet," I told Jane. "But I'm raising some new chicks, and I can't put them with my chickens, so they're going to have to go live at Redwood Farm, by themselves. I'm a little worried."

Jane nodded. "No one wants livestock stolen. But people might need to take care of animals if there's an emergency—like when the creek flooded, or when Agnes died, and people needed to get her chickens to the people who she'd asked to take care of them. Think about it, and then we'll see what we can come up with."

"People would steal Sophie's chickens? For real?" Lupe asked. "I mean, those chicks aren't worth the trouble, are they? Do people steal apples and corn and stuff too?"

"Sometimes, we get problems like that," Jane said. She didn't meet Lupe's eyes.

Which made me wonder: do people around here grow unusual apples and corn? Maybe I should find out more about Chris's mom's vegetable garden.

"The trouble is, anything you can attach to a coop, someone else can take off, one way or another, if they have enough time and no one's watching," Jane continued. "But what if someone was living at Redwood Farm, keeping an eye on things? I mean, you've got a very capable cousin, and there's a whole house there."

Lupe's eyes got even bigger. She didn't say anything.

Part of me wanted Lupe to say no way, she was having too much fun living with us to think about moving. But . . . Jane was right, it would be good if someone was there to keep an eye on my new chicks. Lupe could yell at anyone who threw trash in your yard, no problem. She could probably even stand up to Ms. Griegson, if I explained things.

"Think about it," Jane said. "It's not like you'd be far apart."

Lupe still didn't say anything. Maybe she's tired of living with us already.

Your friend,
Soph

PS Jane gave me samples of three other kinds of chicken treats to try out with my chickens, so she'll know which ones chickens like best. We're going to do a taste test and write some more reviews for her, after I finish the rest of my math homework.

Blackbird Farm

Mariposa García González

Somewhere good, even though I miss her so much

Querida Abuelita,

Lupe didn't bring up moving to Redwood Farm at dinner. Instead, she just talked about the roost stand we're going to build for my new chicks. Mom and Dad were really pleased that Lupe knows how to work all the tools and can teach me how to use them safely.

"I'm so glad you came to stay with us, mija," Mom told Lupe after dinner, squeezing her hand.

I waited for Lupe to say that really she wanted enough space to be able to leave all her bathroom supplies in the bathroom and hang up all her clothes in her room, but she didn't.

Instead, she grinned at Mom. "Me too," she said.

I'd really miss her if she moved.

Maybe she'll just forget Jane ever said anything about it.

Te extraño,

Soficita

EGGSELLENT CRACKED CORN!

This cracked corn is the only treat that will get me out of the nest box I've been hogging all day!

Buffy, Buff Orpington Hen
Blackbird Farm

(Translated from Chicken by
Sophie Brown, poultry farmer)
Sunday, August 31

TASTY, TASTY MEALWORMS!

These dried mealworms are so yummy, I don't want to share them with anyone!

Henrietta, Bantam White Leghorn Hen
Blackbird Farm

(Translated from Chicken by
Sophie Brown, poultry farmer)
Sunday, August 31

BAWKINGLY GOOD PUMPKIN SEEDS!

We love pumpkin seeds! (Especially when they're far away from Buffy and Henrietta!)

The Other Chickens of Blackbird Farm

(Translated from Chicken by
Sophie Brown, poultry farmer)
Sunday, August 31

Monday, September 1

Agnes Taylor
Heaven

Dear Agnes,

Guess what? Lupe heard from her teacher's old student
who did the project on your farm, and he wants to come
visit and tell us about it! His name is Jacob. He's going to
come see us there later this month. I'm so glad we did all
that work to clean up your farm. I wouldn't want him to
be sad when he sees it.

I'm going to have a long list of questions for him,
I bet.

Your friend,
Soph

Blackbird Farm

Wednesday, September 3

Agnes Taylor
Heaven

Dear Agnes,

Today at lunch I told Chris and Sam and Xochi about my trip to Redwood Farm with Lupe. Then I asked Chris if his mom grows unusual vegetables.

"Like kohlrabi?" he asked.

I shrugged. "What's kohlrabi?"

"It's a spiky green or purple vegetable that tastes like a radish but not spicy," Sam told me. "Chris's mom is always giving it to us, because we haven't told her not to yet. You could have some of ours, if you need some. It's okay with ranch dip."

"Is it unusual like my chickens?" I asked.

They all shook their heads. "I don't know of any vegetable that can do things like your chickens," Chris said.

"Me either," Xochi said.

Sam was thinking hard. "People used to say Ms. Winterson's hot peppers would cure any cold you got."

Chris shook his head. "That's just because she was an old lady who lived in a creepy old house and grew her peppers dry, so they were extra spicy. My mom has seeds from hers, and no one says my mom's can cure colds." He looked at me. "Who told you there were vegetables like that?"

So I told them about our conversation with Jane.

"Well, I don't know of anyone growing anything like that," Chris said. "It's too bad, really; my mom would probably like them."

"Maybe there's a catalog you have to write to," I told him.

"Jane's right, you know," Sam said. "Even if Ms. Griegson has learned her lesson, what if something else happened to your chicks, living by themselves?"

"It's a long bike ride too," Chris said. "Do you want to go there every single day to feed them and give them water and check on them? You're going to have to get up really early."

I thought about it. I was really tired when I went to bed last night, just from school and homework and chores, without riding my bike at all. But I didn't tell Chris that. "Of course I will," I told them. "They're my chicks. I have to take care of them."

"But what if you got the stomach flu?" Sam asked. "And you couldn't ride your bike that far?"

"Zookeepers have to teach each other how to take

care of the animals, for when they get sick or have a vacation," Xochi said. "Like substitute teachers."

"Mom or Dad or Lupe would drive me," I told them. "I would take a bucket, so I didn't mess up the car."

Xochi shook her head.

Sam stared at me like I wasn't making any sense. "But why don't you want anyone to live in that house? Don't you trust Lupe?"

"Of course I do!" I told her. "I just . . . I haven't really gotten to spend much time with her yet."

"But you're going to be at Redwood Farm all the time anyway, taking care of your chicks," Chris said.

"It's better if someone is there, if the chicks need help," Xochi said.

"What do your parents think?" Sam asked.

I shrugged. "Lupe didn't bring it up, so neither did I."

"Maybe she doesn't want to live there," Sam said. "Besides, do you really think your parents would let her? I mean, she's too young to live by herself, isn't she?"

"She's eighteen," I told Sam. "Lots of people live by themselves when they're eighteen."

"Nobody I know," Sam said. "Or, only in college dorms or places like that. What if she had boys over?"

"I come over all the time," Chris said.

Sam gave him a look. "Inappropriate college boys."

"Lupe is one of the most responsible people I know," I said. But maybe Sam was still right. Maybe Lupe's parents wouldn't want her to live by herself, and mine would say no way.

"Do you think you could help me build a lower roost for one of my chickens?" Chris asked. "Terminator is getting kind of old, and I think she's having trouble jumping up to the high perch. I don't want her to have to sleep on the coop floor."

"Sure," I told him.

Sam and Xochi wanted to learn to use tools too, so we're all going to build stuff with Lupe. It's going to be great!

Your friend,
Soph

Poultry breed observations by: Sophie Brown,
unusual poultry farmer
Observations made: Friday, September 5
Type of bird: Buff Orpington
Gender of bird: Hen

PLEASE RECORD YOUR NOTES ABOUT THE FOLLOWING:

Comb: pinkish red, small and pointy
Beak: cream
Eyes: orange with black pupils
Wattles: red
Earlobes: red
Beard: nope
Head: golden,
like a golden
retriever
Neck: golden
Body: golden
Tail: golden,
small, points up
Legs and Feet:
cream, no feathers
Eggs: When she's not
broody, Buffy lays big light
brown eggs that sometimes
have a little bit of sand in
them. (You can fish it out
with a spoon before you cook them.)
Typical movements: Walks around, loves to take
dust baths, sometimes hides her head under

comb

earlobe

Super fluffy
poofy like
this

beak

wattle

Chameleon's wing when Henrietta glares at her

Typical vocalizations (if any): For such a mellow chicken, Buffy is really loud. She has to tell the whole world every time someone lays an egg!

Interactions with other poultry:

Buffy is kind of shy. She mostly hangs out with Chameleon and Roadrunner, and doesn't really chase anyone. But when she gets broody and only wants to sit on eggs all day, she puffs up like a huge chicken and gets very fierce—she tries to peck anyone who takes her eggs. Her favorite thing to do is to sit on eggs.

Unusual abilities:

Buffy isn't supposed to have chicks. She had some by accident after Great-Uncle Jim died, and they turned a raccoon to stone. But she's a really nice chicken otherwise.

Needs further research:

Chris agrees that Buffy's abilities are too dangerous to test.

Dear Hort,

You weren't kidding about the mess those chicks make. Good thing I have a barn.

We were building the stand for their new roost today, and at first the noise from the saw and the drill scared them, so they all got quiet and ran and hid under each other in a corner of their box. But then maybe they got used to it or maybe they forgot to be scared, and they started scratching all the wood shavings and everything everywhere and kicking up more dust than ever. They're pretty loud too! And kind of smelly. My friend Sam pointed that out a couple of times, but my friend Xochi said it wasn't as bad as penguins or flamingos. Chris and I didn't really notice, being chicken people, and Lupe is too nice to say anything, if she noticed.

The chicks are growing so fast! Already they would never fit back into eggs. And they're starting to flap their wings around, so it's a good thing we got their roost stand finished. It's perfect! I had no idea you could just build something like that whenever you wanted, out of things no one was using. Why doesn't everyone build stuff all the time?

After we put the tools away, we made sandwiches and took a picnic to the barn at Redwood Farm. I can almost picture the chicks in their new coop, when they're big enough. Chris even pointed out the hook where I could hang up a heat lamp for them if I needed to.

If there's anything else I should plan for, it would be good to know about it now.

Your friend,
Soph

PS How will I know when they're big enough to go live in the coop?

PPS Do you build your perches too? Here is our design, in case yours could use some improvement.

Sophie's chick-Roost Plan:

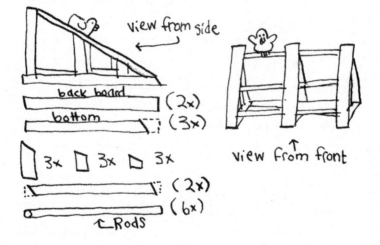

view from side

back board (2x)
bottom (3x)

3x 3x 3x

(2x)
(6x)

Rods

view from front

Date: Sunday, September 7
To: Sophie Brown <unusualchickenfarmer@gmail.com>
From: Hortensia James <hjames@APeculiarKindofBird.com>
Subject: RE: New roost for chicks

Dear Soph,

What a good design! I think it's going to work very well for your chicks.

I usually wait two days after the chicks seem far too big for their box, and one day after I am really sick of all the dust and mess and smell they're creating. That's about three weeks for me, since I move them to a pen that has a heat lamp set up for them. If you need to move them outside without heat, you'll need to wait until they're at least five weeks old. Usually they have some real feathers by then too.

Your friend,
Hort

PS Can you send me another picture of the chick that Chris wanted to call Gandalf, when you have time? I'd like another look at it.

Date: Monday, September 8
To: Hortensia James <hjames@APeculiarKindofBird.com>
From: Sophie Brown <unusualchickenfarmer@gmail.com>
Subject: RE: RE: New roost for chicks

Dear Hort,

Here's another picture, without my thumb this time. I had to wait until that chick was asleep. They move around too much otherwise. I know it looks dead, but don't worry, it isn't.

 Is something wrong with it? I've been really careful to keep them warm and to only feed them the special chick food. But one of the other chicks figured out if they bump into the waterer you sent, sometimes they can knock some water out, and then they all splash around in it. The light gray chick doesn't really splash the way the others do. But maybe it doesn't join in because it's sick?

 Please tell me the truth right away, if it's sick. I will be really sad, but it would be better to know.

Your friend,
Soph

PS It doesn't look sick to me, or act sick.

PPS How do you tell if a chick is sick?

Dear Soph,

No, I don't think anything's wrong with your chick. It sounds like you're taking great care of your new birds. As long as the chicks are moving around, eating, drinking, and pooping normally, I wouldn't worry. I just like to hear about any differences in new chicks, in case it's a new color for that breed and type, or something like that. I'll probably ask you for another photo once the chick has grown up, but there's nothing to worry about.

Thanks for the photo—I think they're adorable when they flop down like that!

Your friend,
Hort

Blackbird Farm

Wednesday, September 10

Jim Brown
Heaven's Barn

Dear Great-Uncle Jim,

Sam was kind of quiet at lunch today. She didn't even really answer Xochi's llama questions—and Sam always wants to talk about llamas. Finally, after Chris asked her for the third time what was up with her, she said, "I don't know. Probably this is way too big a project for us. . . . But maybe, someday—could we build a chicken coop?"

"Are you finally going to get chickens?" Chris asked, staring at her.

Sam shook her head no. "I'm too busy with llamas," she said. "But . . . I think my granddad might miss his chickens. He can't do much these days, but maybe he could watch them."

"Does he live near here?" I asked.

"Yeah, he moved to the retirement home across town," Sam said. "But it's really boring there. People who live there don't all have a lot of energy, but they can still look out the window, and I bet they would like to watch chickens."

194

"I bet you're right," I told her, thinking of when my grandmother was sick.

"We can build whatever you want. But first we need to make sure the people there are okay with having chickens, and that someone can take care of them," Chris said.

"I can ask my cousin," Xochi said. "He works there."

"He does?" Sam asked, surprised.

Xochi nodded. "He helps people there. And he knows how to take care of chickens."

"That would be great," Sam said. "Thanks." She smiled at Xochi—a real smile. "I guess I might need some help getting their chickens set up too."

"Good thing you know some poultry experts, then," I told her, grinning. Who knew that I would become someone people asked for help with chickens? "I bet Lupe would help, and we still have lots of wood and screws and stuff."

You know what, Great-Uncle Jim? I'm glad you left us so many things. Sometimes, they really do come in handy.

Love,
Sophie

PS I bet you miss your chickens too. I hope you can watch them, from wherever you are now. But in case you can't, here's what they did today, with their new friends Aquí and Allí:

Henrietta glared at me until I gave her my apple core.

Roadrunner stole a moth from Chatterbox and ran off with it somewhere. I hope moths are okay for chickens to eat.

Speckles and Freckles had dust baths. They've dug such a big hole, they practically disappear in it when they roll around. I think Chameleon might have been having one too, but it's hard to tell.

Aquí and Allí wanted to lay their eggs in everyone's favorite nest box, but Buffy was already in there and wouldn't get out, even though she wasn't laying eggs, she was just being broody. So they climbed in on top of her, even though there was a perfectly good empty nest box right next to it. I don't know how they all fit. I don't think it was a superpower thing.

After Aquí and Allí laid their eggs and left, Buffy came out for exactly two minutes, drank some water, ate some food, did an enormous stinky poop, and went back in again.

Jim Brown

Heaven's Workshop

Dear Great-Uncle Jim,

I bet when you were alive and went to school here, they
had shop class. But I asked my art teacher about it today,
and he said that even though they still have all the tools
and stuff stored, they don't have any money to have
the class anymore. He said I could start a club, though.
Anyone can, as long as they have a teacher or parent
representative to be part of it. I asked him if he knew
how to build things. He said yes, but he's already helping
with the chorus and the drama club and the band, so he
can't take on a shop club too. I guess everyone's pretty
busy in a small school.

    I don't want to ask my parents. I know they're too
busy already, and then they'll feel bad that they have
to tell me no about something important. Chris's mom
has her hands full too, and Sam's parents have a long
commute, so they couldn't take a break and come over
either.

    Maybe the high school still has shop class. I mean,

I have to learn how to build things somehow, right?

I wish you or Agnes were still alive. I bet you'd be great at building stuff.

Love,

Sophie

Agnes Taylor

Heaven

Dear Agnes,

When I went to check on my chickens today, I thought that Henrietta looked kind of sad, not like her regular self.

Then I saw a huge pile of black feathers, and I freaked out. But Roadrunner ran right up to the bowl where I put their morning treats, and started pecking at the tomatoes with the squishy spots, so I figured she was okay after all.

Only, then, when I really looked at her, I saw she was going bald in patches all over! I could see her skin through her feathers! It was kind of creepy-looking.

I used to worry about what to do if one of the chickens got sick. There are lots of poultry people in this town, and probably even a vet and stuff, but the person that most people ask is Ms. Griegson. And even though she hasn't tried to steal my chickens for a while, I really don't want to ask her for help. I don't want her or anyone else to think she could run Redwood Farm better than me.

I called Chris, since he's been taking care of chickens

for longer than I have. He said he thought Roadrunner was probably fine, just molting.

I read about molting in my chicken books. Apparently it's normal for chickens to lose a whole lot of their feathers in summer or fall. But I didn't know they lost so many they get kind of bald. Chris said I don't need to buy them dog coats or anything, because it doesn't get cold enough here to really be a problem (especially since they're still wearing enough feathers for a chicken-size down jacket).

It still didn't look normal to me, though. So when Gregory came to deliver the mail, I asked him if he could come back after his route and take a look at them. Gregory knows my chickens, so Roadrunner wouldn't surprise him too much if she ran up to say hi.

Today was my lucky day, because it turned out Gregory was due for a fifteen-minute break right then anyway, so he brought his thermal mug of coffee back to take a look at my chickens. He said Chris was exactly right, and pointed out how all of Henrietta's tail feathers had fallen off in the coop, so she looked funny in the back. He tried to show me how the pokey beginnings of feather quills were growing in on Roadrunner, only she sped off again before I could really get a look. I gave him a coffee refill from the pot Mom always has going, and told him thank you thank you thank you, and waved him off on his route again.

I guess this was a good test of what I would do in a chicken emergency. Like an earthquake drill, where they always tell you to have a plan. Well, I can call Chris. He didn't even laugh at me too much. And if it might be a bird thing instead of specifically a chicken thing, I can ask Gregory. And if I absolutely had to, I could even ask Ms. Griegson.

I'm really glad everyone's okay.

Your friend,

Soph

Poultry breed observations by: Sophie Brown, unusual poultry farmer

Observations made: Saturday, September 13

Type of bird: Barred Plymouth Rock

Gender of bird: Hen

PLEASE RECORD YOUR NOTES ABOUT THE FOLLOWING:

Comb: pinkish red, pointy

Beak: yellow, pointy

Eyes: reddish orange with black pupils, I think (Chameleon doesn't like to be stared at)

Wattles: red

Earlobes: red

Beard: nope

Head: black and white striped

Neck: black and white striped

Body: black and white striped

Tail: black and white striped

Legs and Feet: yellow

Eggs: light brown eggs, almost every day (except when she's molting, like right now)

comb

earlobe

beak

wattle

watch close, I'll disappear!!

Typical movements: Chameleon likes to follow me around the barnyard (at a safe distance from Henrietta). She spends a lot of time pecking at the dirt and sitting in the shade.

Typical vocalizations (if any): Chameleon clucks to herself and to Roadrunner, when they're hanging out together. But she never makes a sound when she disappears.

Interactions with other poultry: Roadrunner, Buffy, and Chameleon are pretty good friends. I guess Chameleon doesn't mind cheering Roadrunner on from the sidelines while she runs around.

Unusual abilities:

Chameleon can blend in with her surroundings, like, you know, a chameleon. Only, I guess her abilities don't work that well when she's missing a lot of feathers. When Henrietta tried to charge at her today, Chameleon disappeared, but I could still see patches where she didn't have feathers—and so could Henrietta, because she pecked her right in the bottom. (Don't worry; I reminded Henrietta that is no way to behave.)

Needs further research:

Is it only Chameleon's feathers that change color? Why do they blend in better than her bare chicken bottom?

Collect Chameleon's feathers and try putting them in different places, to see if they change color even when they aren't stuck to her anymore. Maybe I can make a cloak of invisibility out of them!

Nope, they don't work without her—or I don't know how to make them work yet.

Blackbird Farm

Sunday, September 14

Agnes Taylor
Heaven's Best Unusual Poultry Farm

Dear Agnes,

I rode my bike to your farm today, to practice for when my chicks move there. It took a long time, and I was tired when I got home. But that isn't why I'm writing to you.

It's that I found a letter in your mailbox. A letter addressed to me. I don't know how long it's been there.

You know who it was from? Ms. Griegson.

I considered just tearing it up and throwing it out. I didn't want to read whatever she had to say. Maybe she had reasons why she thought it was a good idea to steal my chickens before, but it was still a really mean thing to do to a kid who just moved here.

But then I worried that maybe she'd started stealing my chickens again, and maybe this was a ransom note, or a threat that she was going to do something awful to them if I didn't let her have them.

It wasn't. It was this.

Dear Sophie,

I've been thinking a lot about how Agnes left you her farm and her poultry business. I'm sorry we got off on the wrong foot. I know now that was my fault, and I'd like to try and make it up to you.

I hear that you're beginning to hatch and raise some of her chicks. In case you didn't know, I used to work with Agnes at Redwood Farm. If you run into any issues, please feel free to contact me. I'd like to help.

Sincerely,
Sue Griegson

Dad says it's best to forgive people and move on with your life instead of using all your energy up being mad at them. But Mom says sometimes things really aren't fair, and sometimes being mad helps you understand that they aren't your fault, and that those things should change, not you.

I hope I never have to ask Ms. Griegson for help.

Your friend,
Soph

PS I think I'm going to talk to Lupe about moving to Redwood Farm, now that Ms. Griegson knows I'm raising chicks. It doesn't feel right to leave them there alone with Ms. Griegson for a neighbor, even if she is trying to be nice now.

Blackbird Farm

Monday, September 15

Jim Brown

Heaven

Dear Great-Uncle Jim,

Today at lunch, Xochi told us she asked her cousin Alexis about chickens at the retirement home. He said he didn't know if the manager would let us do it, but that if we set everything up, he would teach some of the other helpers how to feed chickens. He told her he thought the people who live there would really like to watch chickens.

"He likes chickens too," Xochi said.

Sam told Xochi thanks. But she didn't jump in with her lists and everything right away.

"Do you still want to do this?" I asked her.

Sam nodded. But she didn't say anything else.

"Can your granddad ask the manager if it's okay?" I asked.

Sam shook her head no. "Granddad . . . well, he doesn't always know where he is, or what's happening anymore." She looked at the ground. "Maybe he won't even notice or care if there are chickens anyway."

Chris shrugged. "Who knows? Maybe he would really like it. C'mon, Sam—we might as well try asking them.

I can make a drawing of what the coop would look like. Sophie, will you make a list of what they would need and what the duties are?"

I nodded. "Maybe Mom can even help with some research, like how having cats is good for blood pressure or something, only for chickens."

"Alexis and I can make a list of the people and the times and the work," Xochi said.

"A schedule—that's great," I told her. "Thanks." Then I looked at Sam. "I don't want to do the talking, though, okay?" Sam knows that oral presentations make me really nervous. "And your parents would need to buy the chickens and chicken food and all that."

Sam nodded. "Thanks," she said, really quietly.

"If you ask them soon, we could build the coop at Blackbird Farm this Saturday," I told them. "I'll check with Lupe, but it should work."

"I'm going to the zoo on Saturday," Xochi said. "But I will come help when you set up the coop and the chickens, if I can."

"Stop looking so sad," Chris told Sam.

She tried to smile, but she didn't fool any of us really.

I think she still wants to do this, even though she feels sad too. But if she decides she doesn't, at least she knows we were all willing to help her.

Love,
Sophie

Blackbird Farm

Tuesday, September 16

Agnes Taylor

Heaven's Chicken Comedy Club

Dear Agnes,

You know something I never knew when I lived in LA? Chickens can be the funniest animals ever.

Lupe and I hung out with my grown-up chickens this afternoon. Chickens always look kind of serious, because they have beaks and can't smile. But when their feathers are falling out all over the place and some have bare pink bottoms with only one feather left, or spiky new feather quills coming out of the tops of their heads, it makes their expressions extra funny.

Lupe and I gave them all code names, to make them feel better about how silly they look right now.

Freckles, Speckles, and Chatterbox: Plucky, Raggedy, and Patches

Roadrunner: Speedy McNoFeathers

Chameleon: The Tailless Wonder

Buffy: Ms. Porcupine Bottom

Aquí and Allí: Shaggy and Spiky

Henrietta: Quilly Idol (It sounds like Billy Idol—he's

a singer who got famous a long time ago, so you might know him. Lupe showed me pictures of him, and his hair looks just like the spiky quills coming out all over Henrietta! Plus, he always looks kind of mad, just like she does.)

I'm really glad I have chickens.

Your friend,
Soph

Blackbird Farm

Mariposa García González

Heaven

Querida Abuelita,

Today I finally showed the letter Ms. Griegson sent me to Lupe and explained how Ms. Griegson had stolen my chickens before, and how she used to work at Redwood Farm and wanted it for herself, but Agnes left it to me instead, and that's why Jane thought someone should live there.

Lupe frowned, not really mad-frowned, more confused-frowned. "So now she goes around stealing people's chickens? Doesn't anyone call the police or anything?"

"I don't think she steals everyone's chickens. Just mine, because they're from Redwood Farm. Ms. Griegson has a lot of friends here. She's the head of the Poultry Association chapter and is a 4-H leader and runs the poultry show and everything," I told Lupe.

Lupe folded her arms and gave me a look. "Are you sure you aren't worrying a little too much, Soficita? You know people here now too, and they know you."

I looked at my sneakers. I'm starting to get a hole in the toe of one, but my parents haven't noticed, and I'm not bringing it up until I have to. Too bad Great-Uncle Jim didn't leave piles of sneakers in my size around. "Maybe," I told her. "But would you think about living there anyway? If it's not too much trouble?"

So Lupe brought it up at dinner tonight. My parents know that someone tried to steal my chickens, even if they don't know exactly why.

"Is that happening again, Soph? I thought we were all done with that. Do you need me to talk to someone?" Dad asked.

I shook my head. "Jane thought it might be good if someone lived at Redwood Farm, so no one steals stuff from there or dumps more trash in the yard. But if you don't think Lupe should live there, I can bike there every day instead. I don't mind."

Mom frowned. "You're in middle school now, mija. You're going to have more homework, and I don't want these chickens getting in the way of your education." She looked at Lupe. "You'd need to ask your parents how they feel about it, of course."

Lupe nodded. "I thought I'd ask if I could sleep there, but still do my homework and have dinner here, on my way home from college, so I didn't get lonely? And I could still pick Sophie up and drop her off on my way to school."

She didn't say please. She didn't say it was something

she'd like to do. But I think Mom knew it was, because she told Lupe she could ask her parents and see what they said.

I miss her already.

Te extraño,
Soficita

PS Tía Catalina said Lupe and I could have a sleepover at Redwood Farm when my chicks move there, and then she'd think about it.

Blackbird Farm

Thursday, September 18

Agnes Taylor
Heaven's Barn

Dear Agnes,

I guess you probably don't pay much attention to time where you are now, so you might not realize that my chicks are already more than three weeks old! Hort says that's big enough to move into their coop, as long as I set the heat lamp up for them. They're getting way too crowded in their box, and their coop is all ready. I've been practicing riding my bike to your farm and then to school. I get tired, especially with a bunch of textbooks in my backpack, but I can do it.

I was worrying that maybe they'd be scared to move to a new place, or maybe something bad could happen to them there. But then I realized something that made me really happy. You know what? There will be chickens at Redwood Farm again.

I hope that makes you happy too.

Your friend,
Soph

Blackbird Farm

Friday, September 19

Mariposa García González
Heaven

Querida Abuelita,

Lupe and I had a great plan for our sleepover at Agnes's farm. We decided we'd make migas there, and brownies, since Agnes had a bunch of flour and sugar and cocoa powder to use up (and you know I have eggs). We picked which rooms we wanted to sleep in, and put new sheets on the beds and got them all ready. And we checked to make sure the coop was all ready for my pollitos too, with fresh water and plenty of chick food in the feeder and wood shavings in the henhouse.

It was after we hung the heat lamp up and put the chicks in that things went wrong—before we had a chance to make migas, even. It was late afternoon, almost evening, and we were standing outside the coop, hanging out with the chicks, to make sure they felt at home. I was watching the chicks, of course, and Lupe was watching the horses in the field across the road. The light gray chick had gone up into the henhouse by itself, and the others were all trying to stand in the drinking tray of the waterer.

Lupe had just pointed out her favorite horse to me, the one with lots of colors that likes to race around the field almost as fast as Roadrunner. It was rolling around in the dirt. (I always think of horses as being dignified and majestic and expensive-looking, but this one looked ridiculous right then!) We were laughing, and then—

Then I smelled smoke. I didn't know what to say, or what to do. There was sawdust, and straw, and wood everywhere. I didn't know where a fire extinguisher was. I grabbed Lupe's arm, but I couldn't even think what to say.

Luckily, Lupe smelled it too then, and she didn't freeze up like I did. She pulled out her phone. "No signal! Quick—run to the house. Call 911. Tell them fire at Redwood Farm!"

I ran. The 911 lady said they'd send someone right away.

Then I ran back. I know, I should have stayed out of the way and been safe and told the fire people where to go. But Lupe didn't follow me.

When I got to the coop, everything was drenched. I didn't smell smoke anymore. Lupe was holding the empty chick waterer.

When she saw me, she smiled. "It's okay, Soficita. Somehow the shavings in the henhouse caught on fire, but I dumped some water on them and they're out now. It's a good thing you noticed right away. But everything's okay. Shall we go call the fire department to tell them?"

Abuelita, I didn't know what to do. I had a bad feeling that those shavings didn't just catch on fire. "Can you call them?" I asked, and my voice shook a lot. "I just . . . I want to count all the chicks, just to be sure."

Lupe squeezed my arm. "No problem," she told me. "But grab the hose before I go, just in case. I don't know how that happened."

I didn't say anything. I could feel myself shaking, and I didn't want Lupe to notice. I was so scared, and so mad at Hort for not telling me what my chicks could do, and so nervous that the fire department was going to come and say my chicks had to be destroyed. . . . I walked over and grabbed the hose. I turned the knob on the spigot, and took the waterer that Lupe handed me.

"I'll be right back, okay, primita?" She waited until I nodded before she ran up to Agnes's house.

I sprayed down the whole chicken coop, the outside run and inside the henhouse and everything. I filled up the waterer again and counted the chicks. They were all there, and they all seemed fine. The dark brownish-gray ones tried to get right back into the waterer tray, and the light gray one huddled in the corner in some wet shavings. I hoped they weren't too cold, but I couldn't think what else to do.

By the time Lupe convinced the 911 lady that we really didn't need the fire department after all, the mother of one of the firemen had called Joy, the local reporter, and since it was Redwood Farm, she called Mom.

I've never seen Mom and Dad look so scared. Not when Dad lost his job, not even when you told them you were sick. They ran up and grabbed us, and hugged us, and looked at everything all soaking wet, and hugged us some more. For a minute, I thought maybe they could make things all right.

They finally let us go, and Mom asked, "What happened?"

And all my scared feelings came back. I looked at Lupe, and I couldn't say anything. She didn't know about my unusual chickens. But had she guessed my chicks might have started that fire?

You know my mom can always tell when you know more than you're saying. Only, this time, she guessed wrong. Really wrong. Mom looked at Lupe too, and her eyes went from scared to really, really mad, just like that. "Give me your purse, Guadalupe." She held out her hand.

Lupe stared at my mom. "I have no idea what happened," she said. She slowly handed her purse to my mom.

Mom dug through Lupe's purse.

Dad folded his arms and waited.

Then Mom pulled a lighter out of Lupe's purse. She held it up. It said "Hot Stuff" on it, with little flames.

The last time I heard anybody yell like that was when Ms. Griegson tried to steal Henrietta and I blew my whistle.

Only, this time, they weren't yelling at me. They were yelling at Lupe.

"Not even one night away, and this is what you do? You smoke? In front of your prima?" Mom never yells, but she sure was yelling now. "You know what smoking did to your abuela! How could you?"

"I can't believe you'd be so stupid, Guadalupe! We trusted you, and you almost got our daughter killed! You're too responsible for this—this garbage!" Dad doesn't yell either.

Lupe went from confused to mad. "I wasn't smoking! That was a present from a friend—I don't use it! I don't know what happened, but I didn't do it! Ask Sophie!"

I tried, Abuelita. But maybe I didn't try hard enough.

"Lupe wasn't smoking!" I told them.

"Your cousin adores you—she won't tell on you," Mom told Lupe.

I grabbed my parents' hands. "Really, she wasn't smoking!"

"Not where you could see her, maybe!" Mom wasn't done yelling. "Clearly you're not ready to even try out living on your own, Guadalupe. Grab your things and get in our car, Sophie. Guadalupe, you'll drive right behind us, no stops."

"Just because my friends smoke doesn't mean I do!" Lupe said, still mad. "I didn't start a fire, whatever you think."

Mom just pulled me into the car.

I wanted to explain, but I was crying too hard. Or maybe I was just too scared. We drove back to our farm, and Lupe shut herself in her room and won't answer.

I think I know what happened, Abuelita, and Lupe's being blamed for it, but it isn't her fault. But if I tell anyone, they might decide my chickens are too dangerous. So what do I do?

Te extraño,
Soficita

Date: Friday, September 19
To: Hortensia James <hjames@APeculiarKindofBird.com>
From: Sophie Brown <unusualchickenfarmer@gmail.com>
Subject: WHAT WERE YOU THINKING???!!!

Hort, why didn't you TELL me you were sending me fire-breathing chickens????!??!!!

Didn't you ever stop to think I'd need to get things set up specially for them??? That they could burn the whole place down if I wasn't careful????!???!!

Why would you lie to me about them being safe, when they aren't? Are you trying to kill all my chickens and my family?

I'm really, really, really mad at you. Don't bother to write back until you have something to say for yourself.

Ms. Sophie Brown

Date: Friday, September 19
To: Sophie Brown <unusualchickenfarmer@gmail.com>
From: Hortensia James <hjames@APeculiarKindofBird.com>
Subject: RE: WHAT WERE YOU THINKING???!!!

Sophie,

I would never have sent you chicks like that without telling you. I don't know of any chicken breeds that can breathe fire. So we need to figure out what's happening, and fast.

    This is very important. Can you please take photos of the chicks and send them to me, and explain exactly what happened?

    I'm so sorry.

Hopefully still your friend,
Hort

PS Keep everything in the coop wet until we figure this out.

Dear Hort,

I guess it's not your fault that I got a new kind of chicken. I'm sorry I yelled at you. I thought you did it on purpose. But don't you think you should tell people what's going on right up front, so there aren't issues?

What happened is that my cousin and I moved my new chicks to one of the Redwood Farm coops. I'd set it all up with the heat lamp and new wood shavings and everything. When I looked away for just a minute, the wood shavings caught fire. My parents thought my cousin was smoking, and now she's in really big trouble. (They don't understand about unusual chickens.)

I think it's the light gray chick that looks different than the rest. I think it breathes fire. I can't take any pictures right now, because my cousin is in trouble and I can't ride my bike there in the dark. But they look the same as the last photos I sent.

I'll do the best I can to make sure everything in the coop is either wet or nonflammable, but it's not that easy with chicken coops.

What am I supposed to do when this kind of thing happens?

Your friend after all,

Soph

Blackbird Farm

Friday, September 19

Agnes Taylor
Someplace where everything turns out all right

Dear Agnes,

I didn't know things were going to get this complicated. But you know what? When I went out to check on Henrietta and everyone tonight, I remembered how scared I was when Henrietta first moved a jar with her little chicken brain. I never expected anything like that either. For a while, I didn't think I could make it work. But now, we've got our routine, and I don't freak out about her superpowers anymore. Some days I can't find Roadrunner and Chameleon, and I panic a little. I'm really careful with Buffy's eggs, just in case (although she isn't really laying right now, since she's still growing her new feathers back in). And every once in a while, Henrietta gives me a look and I get a little bit worried. But she has never floated me, not one single time.

Maybe things will turn out okay with the new chicks too.

I really hope so.

Your friend,
Soph

Dear Soph,

Thank you so much for sending the information. I want you to know that I need to tell some other unusual chicken people about this. They'll probably send someone out whose job is to learn about new kinds of chickens and to judge if the farmer who's currently raising them can do it safely. I have no doubts about you or how responsible you are! This is just what happens when a new kind of chicken turns up.

Don't worry, just tell the inspector everything you've learned, do your best, and know that whatever happens, you'll have a lot more of Agnes's chickens coming when you're ready.

Your friend,
Hort

PS We haven't had a new kind of chicken that was this unusual in quite a long time—maybe not in my lifetime.

Date: Saturday, September 20
To: Hortensia James <hjames@APeculiarKindofBird.com>
From: Sophie Brown <unusualchickenfarmer@gmail.com>
Subject: Doomed Poultry Farmer (probably)

Dear Hort,

How can I not worry? What kind of inspector is going to let a dangerous new chicken stay with an almost-thirteen-year-old girl? Now I have to wait for someone to show up and decide if I can keep my chick? Great.

I guess you have to do what you have to do. I suppose I'm not exactly mad. But I don't want to email you for a while. I'm really going to miss that new chick, and I bet it's going to miss the other chicks too. I hope you feel bad about that, or you aren't a very good poultry farmer.

Sincerely,
Sophie

Date: Saturday, September 20
To: Sophie Brown <unusualchickenfarmer@gmail.com>
From: Hortensia James <hjames@APeculiarKindofBird.com>
Subject: RE: NOT Doomed Poultry Farmer (probably)

Dear Sophie,

I understand. And I do feel bad about all of this, even though I think I'm doing the right thing.

You know what else? I really, truly believe you can do this.

Please let me know if I can help.

Sincerely,
Hort

236

Blackbird Farm

Saturday, September 20

Mariposa García González
Somewhere Better

Querida Abuelita,

I cried all through my chicken chores this morning.
Buffy let me pet her, but it didn't really make me feel
better. Taking care of chickens isn't always fun.

When I got out my bike to ride to Redwood Farm, my
stomach hurt, a lot. I felt bad leaving without talking
to Lupe first, but she was still in her room, and I had to
check on the chicks. I felt sad all over, the kind of sad that
weighs you down. But, sad or not, I had things I had to do.

As I rode up the road to Redwood Farm, I wished I
could close my eyes. What if another fire had started?
What if it had burnt the whole farm down, maybe even
the farm across the way, and the fields with the horses?
I felt worse and worse and worse.

But when I got there, Redwood Farm looked okay,
and so did the farms around it.

So did my chicks. Everything was still pretty
damp. I guess it wasn't warm enough last night to dry
everything off.

I was so relieved to see those fuzzy little peeping pollitos, I sat down on the path and cried some more—the kind of crying that gets snot everywhere and feels like hiccups you can't stop.

For a minute or two, I wished I was a little kid who never has to make any tough choices. Because I'm not stupid. I'm the owner of Redwood Farm, and I'm the one who has to decide who to tell and what to do.

Dad says that when you can't figure out the big things, try doing any small things you can, and maybe they'll get you moving in the right direction. (Dad's superpower is that he never gives up, even when things seem impossible.)

So I decided to focus on fireproofing the chicken coop today.

First, I cleaned all the wet wood shavings out of the henhouse. It was nasty, but I did it.

Then I started looking for something to put on the henhouse floor instead of shavings—something I could replace or clean the chicken poop off of, that couldn't catch on fire.

Suddenly I heard a noise outside the barn. I ran to see.

It was Chris. "I went to your house so we could get ready to build stuff. Your dad told me you were here," he said. "So I figured I'd come over."

Right, today was building-stuff day. "I forgot," I told him. "Something bad happened."

Here's the thing: Chris knows how dangerous my chickens can be. He knows sometimes you have to make hard choices. I really didn't want to hear him tell me I had to make a hard choice. But I was pretty much at the end of my ideas. I needed help. Chris is my friend, and he loves chickens too. If anyone was going to understand, it was him.

"I think one of the chicks set the wood shavings on fire last night," I told him. "My parents are really mad, but they're mad at Lupe for starting a fire. They don't know."

Maybe I hoped Chris would just shrug and say, "Oh yeah, I guess it was one of those chickens. Here's how Agnes always took care of them."

But he didn't. His mouth fell open. He didn't say anything for almost a whole minute. That never happens with Chris.

I tried to just breathe through it, the way Mom tells me to, but the heavy sad welled right up and started me crying again.

Chris took one look at me and ran, leaving me there by myself.

I couldn't believe he'd do that to me. Not now; not when we were real friends. Was he going to tell my parents without even talking to me first? Was he going to come back with a bunch of people with pitchforks and do a Frankenstein riot to me and my chicks?

I grabbed Agnes's pitchfork. It was heavy and spiky

and taller than me, but it felt better to hold something in my hands. At least I wouldn't be the only person without a pitchfork. Then I went to guard my chicks.

Chris found me there a couple of minutes later. He didn't bring a riot or a pitchfork. I tried to yell at him and wave the pitchfork, but I was crying too hard.

"Whoa, Soph," he said, stepping back. "I called Sam. She's on her way. We'll figure it out. Just—stop crying. And maybe put that thing down?"

I stared at him for a minute, still sniffing. Chris didn't leave me to figure it out by myself, and he didn't bring a riot. He called for backup.

I handed him the pitchfork.

Chris leaned the pitchfork up in a corner. "Okay," he said. "What's the plan?"

I shrugged. If I knew what the plan was, I wouldn't be just standing there.

Chris opened the door to the coop and went in, closing it carefully behind him. "Okay, everything's damp, nothing's going to burn for now. So we need to start a list, because you know Sam's going to want one anyway when she gets here."

I tried to clear my throat, but my voice still wobbled. "I was trying to find something to put in there that wouldn't burn."

Chris nodded, ignoring my wobbly voice. "Step one: find some dirt or gravel or something. Step two: put it in the henhouse."

He came back out of the coop. "Okay, let's go look in the bins." He grabbed the pitchfork and carried it back to the barn.

When Sam got there, we'd found a bin of gravel and were carrying it in buckets to the henhouse.

Sam nodded at Chris and me. "Have you examined the coops to see which one Agnes might have kept chickens like that in?" she asked.

Chris's eyebrows went up. "Not yet," he said.

We looked around at the coops.

"They all have wood frames," Sam told me.

My heart sank. "Did Agnes have chickens like these?"

Neither of them looked at me.

"Not that I ever heard of," Sam said.

Chris was still examining the coops. "What about that one?" he asked. He was pointing at a coop almost like all the others, with a wood frame and wire mesh all around it, and a wooden henhouse in the top part, with a ramp going up. But this one didn't have any wood shavings on the ground, only dirt, and the run had a big shallow hole in the ground. "Agnes's duck coop?"

"Can you put chickens in a duck coop?" I asked.

Chris shrugged. "Sure. We could put a metal pole in the shade for them to roost on, and we could probably find something for the ramp that wouldn't burn."

Sam nodded. "It could work," she said. "Chris, see if you can find a metal pipe, and something for a ramp."

She grabbed Chris's buckets of gravel and started walking toward the duck coop.

Sam and I put gravel over the wooden floor of the duck house and stapled tinfoil on the walls, while Chris dragged a couple of long metal tubes and a piece of sturdy wire fence out and sang songs about working on the chain gang and in coal mines. (Normally Sam would have pointed out there are no coal mines on Agnes's farm, but today, she didn't.)

Sam figured out how to attach a long metal tube to the coop walls so that it wouldn't spin around when a chick hopped on it and throw the chick off. Chris figured out how to remove the old wooden ramp and put the narrow piece of wire fence in, and how to attach it so it wouldn't fall off. It's a good thing that my friends already know how to make do with what you have around.

I filled up the hole with a little bit of water to make a pond, even though I was putting chickens in there, not ducks, because it couldn't hurt to have some water around if we needed it. Then Chris bailed some of it out, to be sure the chicks couldn't drown themselves in it, since they aren't exactly babies anymore but they aren't old enough to have any sense yet.

Chris stacked concrete blocks up in front of the wooden frame posts, high enough so the chicks couldn't set them on fire. Then Sam pushed on them to make sure they couldn't fall over and crush anyone.

Sam measured the distance between the gravel on the ground of the coop and the wooden duck house bottom above it. It was three feet.

"How far can the chicks shoot flames?" she asked.

I shrugged. "I don't know. I've never seen them do it."

"Do they breathe fire, or shoot fire out of their eyeballs, or move matches with their minds, or what?" Chris asked.

"I don't know, okay?" I guess I snapped a little.

They were both quiet for a while, long enough that I remembered that they were both here helping me with something scary, something that didn't have to be their problem. "I'm sorry," I said. "I'm just worried."

Sam nodded. "Chris, you drag the hose back here and turn it on. Squirt down the whole coop, just in case anything flammable is in range. Sophie, we're going to figure out how to move the chicks from the coop they're in to this one as safely as we can."

I nodded. Chris went to get the hose, and Sam and I went to look at the chicks.

We stared at them in silence for a while. They weren't trying to set anything on fire, just doing what they always do: trying to sit in the water dish (the dark brownish-gray ones) and watching from a corner (the light gray one).

"Do you think they're trying to make themselves fireproof?" Sam asked.

I just shrugged.

Then Sam said, "We could really use a rabbit cage."

Chris ran over from the duck coop. "I didn't see one anywhere. But there's a plastic dog crate in the barn."

"Does plastic burn?" I asked.

"Sort of," Sam said. "It mostly melts, and it gives off noxious fumes that are bad for you and the earth. But it doesn't catch on fire like paper or wood, or at least it doesn't at normal fire temperatures."

"Do these chickens have superheat-force abilities?" Chris asked.

I shrugged again. I didn't think any words could get past the lump in my throat anymore, so why try?

"All right, team," Chris said, standing tall and sticking out his chest. "We are about to attempt a dangerous maneuver. If we fail, terrible—" He looked at my face and stopped. "Uh, right. We're just going to put the chicks in the dog crate and move them to the duck coop, and everything will be fine."

We left Chris to watch the chicks. Sam and I went to the barn and found the dog crate, a wheelbarrow to move it in, some safety goggles, four mismatched oven mitts, two pairs of long barbecue tongs, some tinfoil, and a jar full of sunflower seeds.

We wheeled everything back to the chicken coop.

"No signs of unusual activity," Chris reported, putting his goggles and oven mitts on.

Sam wrapped tinfoil around Chris's oven mitts and then around mine, so they wouldn't catch on fire. The crinkle of the tinfoil sounded really loud in the sudden quiet. "There aren't enough mitts for everyone, so I'll be the backup, since you two know more about chickens." She took a pair of barbecue tongs and put her goggles on. "Now bring the crate in, put the sunflower seeds inside, wait until all the chicks are inside, latch the crate, and lift it into the wheelbarrow. I'll drive."

I took a deep breath.

Chris just opened the coop door and took the crate in.

I dumped the sunflower seeds into the crate. Then I got back by the door.

Chris was trying to herd the chicks toward the crate.

"Get away from them, Chris!" Sam yelled. "You're wearing shorts! They're going to burn you!"

Chris stepped back, but not very far. The chicks ran around in circles and fell over in little wet piles for a minute. Then a chick noticed the open crate and rushed inside.

All the dark brownish-gray chicks followed it. I looked around. Where was the light gray chick?

Very carefully, I swung the big cleaning door of the henhouse open, just as the light gray chick shot a tiny stream of fire from its beak.

Chris stared. "That's it?" He pulled off his oven mitts and picked up the chick. It peeped at him, struggling in his hand. "I've seen bigger flames on a match." He put the light gray chick in the crate, and shut the door.

"Matches are dangerous too!" Sam told him.

"Sure, but not like a blowtorch," Chris told her. "Grab the feeder and the waterer, Soph. It's going to be fine." Then he carried the crate to the duck coop.

I grabbed the waterer and handed the feeder to Sam. We followed him.

We set the feeder and waterer up in the duck coop while Chris set the crate down. He opened the door and stepped back.

One of the dark brownish-gray chicks stepped cautiously out. It saw the pond, and made a run for it. The rest of the dark brownish-gray chicks followed.

Chris made a funny noise. "They're swimming," he said.

I shrugged. "So?"

Chris watched the brownish-gray chicks paddle around. "Chickens' feathers aren't waterproof, Soph. They get all soggy, and chickens don't float, so they can't swim." He stared at the chicks. "Well, normal chickens can't swim."

The light gray chick crept out after them. It stepped on the wet gravel, picked its foot up again, and shook it. A tiny flame shot from its beak.

Slowly, I sank down onto the path. "We need to make

some observations here. Sam, can you find us some pencils and paper?"

Sam nodded, and took off for the barn.

We sat and ate the apples Sam picked and recorded our observations for at least an hour. Nothing caught on fire. No one got hurt. I collected all the research, and I told Chris and Sam thanks, that I was okay now, and I was going to go home.

Sam bit her lip. "What are your parents going to do to Lupe?" she asked. "Are you going to tell them about your chicks?"

I watched the chicks for a minute or so, storing the memory up in my mind, in case things got bad again. The dark brownish-gray chicks were still paddling around the pond, not caring at all that chickens don't do that. The light gray chick was fast asleep, looking just like the regular chicks in Jane's feedstore.

Then I met Sam's eyes. Just because you don't want to do something doesn't mean it isn't the right thing to do. "I have to tell them. It isn't fair to Lupe to let them think she did something bad. Besides, they need to know, just in case something bad does happen."

Sam nodded. So did Chris.

We walked along the path to where our bikes were parked.

Sam gave me a hug. "Call us if you need something. We'll help."

Chris nodded.

"Sorry about the pitchfork," I told him.

He grinned. "We might have to put that in a comic someday."

I wasn't up to laughing yet. But at least it made me smile.

The whole bike ride home, I thought about how I'd tell my parents and Lupe. I'd start by explaining about the chicks. Then I could tell them about my other chickens. They'd be amazed, of course, but they'd start to finally understand why Redwood Farm was important. They'd probably be pretty impressed by how responsibly I'd dealt with things, even though they might be kind of mad I hadn't told them all the details. But I could explain they'd been pretty busy, and they could tell me they were never too busy to help me with important things.

I'm scared. But I'm going to tell them now.

I know you're dead, but please cross your fingers for me anyway, Abuelita.

Te extraño,
Soficita

Poultry breed observations by: Sophie Brown, unusual chicken farmer

Observations made: Saturday, September 20

Type of bird: Brownish-gray chicks. No idea yet—they look like half the chicks at the feedstore

Gender of bird: Too soon to tell, Chris says

PLEASE RECORD YOUR NOTES ABOUT THE FOLLOWING:

Comb: none yet

Beak: yellow

Eyes: black

Wattles: none yet

Earlobes: I can't see them yet

Beard: none yet

Head: yellow on top

Neck: yellowish brownish gray

Body: brownish gray

Tail: chicks don't really have tails yet

Legs and Feet: pinkish-yellowish toes, with brownish-gray fluff. They're really small, so it's hard to tell, but we think there might be webbing between their toes.

Eggs: Not yet!

Typical movements: They paddle around in a puddle a lot, and try to sit in the waterer or wet shavings. Otherwise they just eat, sleep, and poop.

comb
earlobe
beak
wattle

Not like this, more like THIS

Typical vocalizations (if any): They peep like any other chicks.

Interactions with other poultry: They don't seem scared of the light gray chick. Sometimes they hang out together, when they're not swimming.

Unusual abilities: They can swim, I think? Their feathers might be waterproof, and they can float.

Light gray chick:

Same as above, except light gray for the brownish-gray parts. Even its toes look the same. So maybe it could swim, if it wanted to? Or, maybe it isn't webbing after all. I'll try to observe the chicks' toes at the feedstore so I know what regular chick toes look like.

Typical movements: Doesn't play in water or swim like the others. Eats, sleeps, poops like other chicks. Sometimes very small flames come out of its beak. Afterward, it rubs its beak on its shoulder fluff, like my big chickens do when they eat something messy.

Interactions with other poultry: HAS NOT SET ANY CHICKS ON FIRE. Or even come close. At least not while I was watching. Hangs out with the other chicks when they're not swimming.

Unusual abilities: Breathes flames 1/2 inch long (that's an estimate). But not at other chicks, not even when they bump into it or step on it while it's asleep. Honestly, I have no idea what makes it do that. Neither do Chris and Sam.

Needs further research: Everything

Blackbird Farm

Saturday, September 20

Mariposa García González
Heaven

Querida Abuelita,

I told Mom and Dad about my chicks, just like I planned.

The problem was that they didn't believe me.

Mom gave me a hug. "Mija, I know you love your prima and want to help her. But when Lupe does something she shouldn't, she has to deal with the consequences, just like you do."

"But Lupe didn't do anything bad!" I told them again. "Lupe put out the fire that my chick started. She acted right away when I got scared. She saved us."

Dad gave me a look. "Right. From the fire-breathing chick."

"No, from the fire it started," I told him. "Come see it yourself! Or ask Chris and Sam—they saw it too!" My voice wobbled, but I couldn't give up.

Mom hugged me harder. "Honey, I'm glad you've found true friends here. I'm impressed with your imagination, and I know your chickens are special to you, but no fire-breathing chick can get Lupe out of trouble."

"There's no need to make things up to help her. We're not going to send her back to LA," Dad said.

I pulled away. "I'm not making things up," I told them. "I'm telling you the truth, even though I didn't want to, because it's the right thing to do." I could feel tears burning my eyes. "I can't make you believe me. But I'm going to tell Lupe too. She deserves to know."

I turned and ran up the stairs before the tears went everywhere.

Lupe was sitting on her bed, staring at the stacks of boxes. "Hey, primita," she said when I burst in. Then she saw my face, and she got up to give me a hug. "What's wrong?"

It all gushed out, how scared I was for my chicks, how I knew I should have spoken up but I hadn't, how it was all my fault, what my chicks could do, how I told my parents but they didn't believe me.

Lupe didn't push me away or tell me to go clean myself up, even though I was a big dripping snotty mess. She just hugged me until I was done.

I stepped back. "Are you mad?" I asked her, sniffing, looking down at my sneakers.

"I'm not mad at you, Soficita," Lupe said. "I'm kind of mad at the situation. It sucks to be blamed for something you didn't do, and to have people you normally respect thinking you're irresponsible and lying."

I nodded. "I'm sorry."

She handed me a tissue. "Your parents have assigned me twenty hours of community service."

"I'll help," I told her. "I'll do the work with you, or I can do it for you."

Lupe shook her head. "You can do whatever you want, but I'm not lying to your parents, and I'm not letting you do the work they assigned me, whether it was fair or not. That's between me and them."

"I just want to make things right," I said. "I feel sick in my stomach, and I don't know how else to fix it."

"You don't fix something that's wrong by doing something else that's wrong—Abuelita taught us that," she told me. "You fix it by doing things that are right. Sometimes it's still not enough, but at least you know you tried."

I nodded. "Sometimes it's just hard to remember," I said, and my voice went funny when my eyes filled up again. "Especially when people don't believe you tried."

"I think I better take a closer look at these chicks of yours," Lupe said, grabbing her purse and her keys.

Mom and Dad weren't exactly happy that Lupe and I were going to Redwood Farm. But they didn't try to stop us.

They didn't want to come with us either, though.

Nothing had changed much since I was there. Nothing was on fire. None of the concrete blocks had fallen on anyone and squashed them. The dark brownish-gray chicks were still swimming around in the puddle. The light gray chick was taking a nap next to an apple core.

"Hey, pollitos," I called softly. "My cousin Lupe is here to say hi."

The dark brownish-gray chicks didn't pay any attention. The light gray chick didn't wake up.

I sat down on the path to wait. Lupe sat down next to me.

"Chris says regular chickens can't swim. Their feathers aren't waterproof, so they can't float," I told Lupe after a while.

We watched the dark brownish-gray chicks paddle around.

One of them walked out of the pond and ran over toward the feeder. The rest followed. I held my breath when they jostled the light gray chick.

Slowly it got up. It looked at me, took a few steps, and opened its beak.

A tiny flame shot out.

Lupe grabbed my hand and held it tight.

The light gray chick wandered back to the apple core and began pecking at it.

"Maybe it's a new species?" Lupe said.

I shrugged. "Maybe. Hort says none of the parent chickens breathe fire."

Lupe took a deep breath. She let it out, very slowly. "Okay. So the problem is that you have a fire-breathing chicken. What do we need to do?"

I shook my head. "The problem is that farms are flammable, not that I have a chicken with a new superpower."

Lupe thought that over. "You guys did a good job making everything fireproof," she said. "I'm glad your friends helped you. It's only breathing small flames now, but that's still pretty scary. People could get hurt if this doesn't work."

"Right," I said. "Hort told the unusual chicken inspectors that they have to come check things out. If they don't think I can keep it safely, they'll take my chick away."

"Don't you want them to?" Lupe asked.

I stared at the light gray chick. "I want to try to keep it safely here with its family."

"Okay," Lupe said. Her voice was only a little shaky now. She took a few deep breaths. "When we have a problem, we ask ourselves who the helpers are."

"Chris and Sam helped me today," I told her.

She nodded. "Who else? Who knows the most about chickens, or about these chickens?"

"The inspectors might know the most, I guess, but I don't know how to reach them," I told her. "Hort and Betty know way more than I do. But I can't mail a chick that's going to burn up the box, and I don't want to give my chick away."

Lupe nodded. "Okay. Who here knows the most about chickens?"

"Ms. O'Malley knows a lot," I told her. And even though my stomach was twisting all around, I added, "And Ms. Griegson. She knows a lot about chickens, she has a dangerous kind herself, and she trained here with Agnes."

"Is she a helper?" Lupe asked me.

I put my brain on its "what is fair" setting. "She's a helper to chickens. But she hasn't been a helper to me."

"So this Ms. Griegson has the expertise, but she might think she'd be the better person to raise your chick." Lupe sat up straight and put her thinking-hard face on.

"She can't," I told her. "Agnes didn't trust her judgment."

"I'm not giving your chick away, Soficita," Lupe said. "But we have to problem-solve so the inspectors won't take it, right?"

I looked down at the hole in my sneaker, and nodded. "Sometimes I try so hard, and then things still don't work out. Probably they're going to take my chick anyway. Maybe I should just let them."

I looked up just as the light gray chick let out another tiny burst of flame, then rubbed its beak on its shoulder, like it was wiping its nose. I held my breath as it wandered over to the other chicks. But it only joined the crowd at the feeder, pecking at the chick food. I guess it's a good thing the other chicks are always covered in water, since they didn't move away from it.

"Look, Soph. I don't want to scare you," Lupe said. "But you know that if they decide that chick is too dangerous for you, they might not let you keep your other chickens either. I mean, you have a chicken that turns people to stone, right?"

"Only her chicks can do that—and I don't have a rooster, so she can't have chicks. And only raccoons, maybe, not people," I told her. But my heart was pounding now. There was no way I was going to sit back and let them take ALL my chickens. "Okay. What do we do next?"

"Maybe you should talk to this Ms. Griegson," Lupe said. "Ask her what you need to know, and see what she says."

I sighed. "Maybe. But Ms. Griegson makes me nervous. So how am I going to ask her everything I need to, and then remember her answers too?"

Lupe squeezed my hand. "Could you write her a letter instead? What do you need to know from her?"

I thought hard. "Whether Agnes ever had a chicken like this, or was trying to breed one. What Agnes did when a new kind of chicken hatched."

Lupe nodded. "Good questions. Do you think she'll answer them truthfully?"

I knew Ms. Griegson loved unusual chickens, even if she didn't like me. "Yeah, she will. It's just that once she finds out, she might do everything she can to take my chick, or all my chickens. What if she tells my parents it isn't safe for me to keep them?"

"Well, you already told your parents yourself what this one can do," Lupe said. "Maybe they would believe her. But what if we did everything we could first to make things safe? Then the town wouldn't really be any safer if she had it, right?"

I nodded slowly.

"We need an expert on fire prevention—someone Ms. Griegson and your parents respect. Let's find a fireman," Lupe said, getting up.

"Okay. We'll start at the library," I told her. Ms. O'Malley knows everyone and who does what, and they all listen to her.

When I told Ms. O'Malley that I was raising new chicks and was worried things might catch on fire, her eyes went wide for a moment. But she nodded. "Yes, you'd better go to the fire department and talk to Al Tomei. Try after two o'clock today. Just say that I sent you, that you inherited Redwood Farm's chickens, and that it's important that the department give you whatever help they can, as soon as possible."

I nodded.

"It's just down the street, across from the thrift store," Ms. O'Malley said.

"Thanks." I looked down at her desk and gathered up my courage. "I'm going to ask Ms. Griegson if she knows anything that could help me. But, uh, if you hear her telling people that I don't know how to take care of my chickens, would you let me know?"

Ms. O'Malley put her hands on her hips. "Sophia Brown, you have checked out every single chicken book in this library multiple times. Agnes left her farm to you. Who would be better prepared than you to care for your chickens?" She folded her arms. "If you have any more problems with Sue Griegson, you come straight to me."

As we drove home to have some late lunch before dealing with the fire department, Lupe turned to me. "You know, Soficita, a lot of people here do respect you. That librarian really thinks you can do this."

I nodded. When I moved here, I didn't think Ms. O'Malley would ever be someone who had my back. But now I think she'd do her best to help me. I don't think there's much she could do about an unusual chicken inspector, though. "I guess they respect me because Agnes trusted me with her chickens," I told her.

Lupe squeezed my hand. "Well, I knew you first, and I think you can do it too."

I wish you were here, Abuelita. I know you would believe me. But since you can't be with us, I'm really glad Lupe is here.

Te extraño mucho,
Soficita

CHICKEN AWARD

THIS CHICKEN AWARD IS PRESENTED TO

FRECKLES

FOR LETTING ME PICK HER UP AND GIVE HER A HUG,
EVEN THOUGH SHE HATES HUGS. THANKS FOR NOT
POOPING ON MY SHOES THIS TIME.

Sophia Mariposa Brown

Sophia Mariposa Brown, unusual poultry farmer
Saturday, September 20

Blackbird Farm

Saturday, September 20

Mariposa García González

Heaven

Querida Abuelita,

Lupe and I went back to town this afternoon.

Al Tomei turned out to be an Asian lady with short gray hair and lots of muscles who was wearing a fire-department uniform. I told her what Ms. O'Malley told me to say, and she didn't freak out, but she did start moving very quickly. She yelled at someone named John to take over for her, asked if we needed the ladder truck, and nodded when Lupe explained that we needed a safety consultation. She told us to meet her at Redwood Farm.

When we got there, we found Al watching the light gray chick breathe little spikes of flame. She still wasn't freaking out. I took that as a good sign.

"That's the potential threat?" Al nodded at the light gray chick.

I stood up as straight and tall as I could. "No. That's one of my new chicks that just hatched. It's not a threat. We just need to make sure it doesn't cause any accidents."

Al thought about that for a moment, and nodded. "Good thing you came to me, then." She examined the duck coop carefully. "Nice setup," she said, and I started to breathe again. "Are you going to let it out of the coop?"

I bit my lip. "Well, I'd like to, when it's older. But not until we learn more about it."

Al nodded. "We can do a reevaluation later, to make certain there's no areas of concern. So, for now, we just need to concentrate on the area around the coop, in case its range increases or anything unexpected happens. Correct?"

Lupe was staring at Al. "Have you done this before?" she asked.

Al looked at Lupe and grinned. "You're new here," she said. Then she looked at me. "Agnes was a good friend," she told me. "The safety of the community is my main concern, but as long as your setup is safe, we're good."

She pulled a brochure from her pocket and handed it to me. "Let's go over how to make a fire-safety zone surrounding the coop. You can use our safety recommendations for farm welding shops as a model— this chick doesn't have nearly the heat or range of a welding torch. We'll go over what you need to do, and then I'm going to give you a week to get things set up. Next weekend, I'll come back out to inspect for any risks we might have missed."

I nodded. "Thanks. I appreciate it."

"Thank you for coming to me. It's good to be at Redwood Farm again," she said.

Creating a fire-safety zone meant pulling up dead plants and spreading more gravel in the area that Al helped us measure out. The brochure had a checklist, and it felt good to look down the list and know that we were doing everything we could to keep everybody's farms from burning up.

Al got us started, then gave us her card and went back to the fire station.

"Feel better?" Lupe asked, stopping to stretch.

"Kind of," I told her, squishing down the dead plants in the bucket so I could fit more in. "I just want to know that everything will be okay, so I can stop worrying."

Lupe shook her head. "Soficita, no one ever really knows that. Not for sure. The best we can do is to try our hardest." She smiled. "I'm pretty sure you're trying your hardest."

I didn't feel like smiling, though. What if there's something I could be doing that I haven't thought of yet? Maybe that gray chick is the only one in the world with that superpower. What if I can't keep it safe?

It used to be easy to know what was right and to try my best to do it. So why is it so hard now?

Te extraño,
Soficita

Blackbird Farm

CHICKEN AWARD

THIS CHICKEN-KEEPER AWARD IS PRESENTED TO

SOPHIA MARIPOSA BROWN

Sophie!

Super
H.

FOR WORKING SO HARD TO KEEP HER UNUSUAL
CHICKENS SAFE. I'M SO PROUD OF YOU, PRIMITA.

Guadalupe Isabella Hernandez
Saturday, September 20

Blackbird Farm

Sunday, September 21

Jim Brown
Heaven

Dear Great-Uncle Jim,

I felt bad we didn't build a chicken coop for the place where Sam's granddad lives, like we'd planned to yesterday. So I asked Lupe if she would help us build one today instead.

Lupe sighed. "I wish I could, but I have to figure out where I can volunteer for the hours your parents are making me do. Do you know anyone that might want a brilliant teacher-in-training to help them out?"

I thought for a minute. And then I had my best idea ever. "Yes! I want to start a building-stuff club at my school, but we need a teacher or parent to lead it, and no one has time. Would you be our leader?"

"Well, I'm not exactly a teacher, and I'm not a parent. . . ." Then Lupe grinned. "But if your school would make an exception for me, it would be so fun! I bet I could even do one of my education presentations on the experience."

"I think they'd make an exception, especially if it was for college!" I said.

"Then I guess we'd better go build that coop and take some pictures, so they can see my skills!" Lupe said, smiling. "I do have one condition, though. You have to actually write to Ms. Griegson, like we talked about."

I don't want to write to her. But Lupe is right, and I told her so. I'll do it next, and I'll put it in the mail first thing tomorrow.

Love,

Soph

PS It's going to be the best coop ever. And the best club ever too!

PPS I really, really, really, really don't want to write to Ms. Griegson.

Sunday, September 21

Sue Griegson
Briar Farm

Ms. Griegson,

Thank you for writing to me and offering to help. I do
have some questions.

1. Do you know if Agnes was trying to breed new
   kinds of unusual chickens?
2. What did Agnes do when a new kind of chicken
   hatched?

It's okay if you don't know the answers. Other people
are helping me too.

Sincerely,
Sophie

PS Did you ever meet the unusual poultry inspectors?
What did Agnes do when they came?

Ms. Sophie Brown
Redwood Farm

Dear Sophie,

Thank you for writing to me. I promise to tell you everything I know, but unfortunately it isn't much.

1. If Agnes was trying to breed any new varieties of chicken, she never told me about it. Redwood Farm was for continuing existing breeds and making them available to poultry farmers who could care for them and appreciate them.
2. As far as I know, Agnes never hatched any new breeds, only the occasional color variation.

Please let me know if there's anything else I can do to help you.

Sincerely,
Sue

PS I didn't finish my apprenticeship with Agnes. And I've never even heard of an unusual chicken inspector. I'm sorry.

UNUSUAL POULTRY COMMITTEE, NORTHERN CALIFORNIA DIVISION

Tuesday, September 23

Ms. Sophie Brown
Redwood Farm
Gravenstein, CA 95472

Dear Ms. Brown,

I am requesting permission for an observational visit to Redwood Farm this Saturday, September 27, at 2:00 p.m., in order to obtain additional information for an important upcoming Committee decision.

I believe you've already been informed about this possibility, but if you will not be able to be present for this appointment, or if you have additional questions, please feel free to contact the division secretary at (707) 578-8938. Otherwise, I'll see you at Redwood Farm on Saturday.

Sincerely,
Inspector Lee

Date: Thursday, September 25
To: Hortensia James <hjames@APeculiarKindofBird.com>
From: Sophie Brown <unusualchickenfarmer@gmail.com>
Subject: RE: RE: NOT Doomed Poultry Farmer (maybe) (if I'm really lucky)

Dear Hort,

The inspector is coming this Saturday. I'm trying hard not to be mad at you. I've been working with the fire department to do my best to make everything safe.

Just thought you might want to know.

Soph

Friday, September 26

Jim Brown

Farmhalla

Dear Great-Uncle Jim,

There's no point in moping around, waiting for inspection day. So I've been keeping busy.

Yesterday afternoon we took the chicken coop we built to the retirement home. Xochi's cousin Alexis showed us where to set it up. He's about Lupe's age, and he works there helping people during the day, and goes to nursing school at night. He has a black ponytail and dark brown skin and a really great smile. I bet Lupe wished she wore her cute jeans instead of her building-stuff jeans.

It took us a while, but we got everything set up. Lupe made sure the coop was stable, and Xochi helped Sam put the new chickens inside, and Chris organized the supplies, and I thumbtacked the schedule to the coop wall, so everyone would know when it was their turn to feed the chickens.

There was a little boy visiting somebody with his dad who kept watching us through the window. Alexis went in to ask if they wanted to come out and meet the chickens. That boy must have opened and shut the little egg-collection door about twenty times. Finally, the dad said they had to go, but maybe they could come back tomorrow and see the chickens again. That kid looked like someone told him he could go to the zoo!

The receptionist took a photo of all of us standing in front of the new coop, with the "Welcome Chickens" sign their art class made. The kitchen staff have been collecting scraps that are good for chickens, and Alexis already made sure everyone on the schedule knows how to feed the chickens and change their water and collect their eggs. (Sam gets to clean the coop.)

"It's no problem," Alexis told us when Sam told him how much she appreciated it. But Sam's going to make cookies for them all anyway.

I'm glad I got to work on this. Now Sam's granddad can watch chickens, and so can Sam, when she goes to visit him there, and Alexis can when he's at work too. I'm already thinking about who else could probably use a chicken coop. Any place where people have to wait around would love one, I bet, as long as someone can take good care of the chickens.

Love,
Soph

Blackbird Farm

Saturday, September 27

Agnes Taylor

Heaven

Dear Agnes,

Today Lupe helped me pick out the right poultry-farmer outfit. Then we picked up all my friends and drove to Redwood Farm to get things ready for the inspector's visit.

Al came at one-thirty to check the fire-safety zone. She said it looked good, and she signed a form for me to put on the coop so the inspector could see it.

Lupe and Chris kept an eye out for the inspector while Sam and Xochi and I went back to see the chicks. Their real feathers are growing in, but they still make the cutest peeping noises! I watched them for a minute and let myself pretend everything would be okay. I really thought I believed it too. I don't know why I cried anyway.

Then Xochi gave me a hug, and Sam gave me a tissue and said, "You did your best, Soph. Let's go see if the inspector's here."

As we were crossing the picnic spot, I heard the front

gate clink open, then shut. I froze. We waited for the inspector to come through Agnes's front hedge.

Instead, Ms. O'Malley's nephew appeared. "Hi," he called out, stopping when he saw us. "It's nice to see you again."

Lupe grabbed my arm. "It's Jacob!" she whispered. "I'm so sorry, Soph—I forgot about his visit!"

"You did a project on Redwood Farm for college?" I asked him.

He nodded, smiling. "My friends call me Jake."

I checked my watch. We still had fifteen minutes before the inspection. I looked at Lupe.

Lupe nodded, and I knew that when the inspector arrived, she'd show Jake around some other part of the farm while I took care of business.

Chris was staring at Jake. "What kind of project did you do with Agnes?" he asked.

"4-H stuff, mostly—Agnes was my 4-H leader," Jake said. "Then, at college, I did an analysis for Professor Shaw's class on business plans for specialty mail-order poultry businesses. I'm guessing that Professor Shaw found it more interesting than you will, but thanks for letting me come visit, anyway."

"I think it sounds fascinating!" Lupe told him.

Xochi rolled her eyes and grinned at me. (Jake was pretty cute.)

"Thanks," he told Lupe, smiling. "So, can I have a

tour? You guys sure got a lot of work done on this place since I saw it last. Looks like your picnic worked out well!"

So Sam told him all about the dance party at the picnic, since he'd had to leave early to go deliver more pizzas, and what we got done, and how everybody liked his dad's pizza.

"Did you move all this gravel here then too?" Jake asked, pointing at the fire-safety zone.

"No, we still had work to do after the picnic," Chris said. "Agnes couldn't keep everything up herself, so there was a lot to do, like making this fire-safety zone around that coop. But we got it done."

Jake nodded. "I saw lots of people working on the coops that day," he said, starting toward them. "They look great! I remember the clucking when Agnes had them all full of chickens—it sounded like the zoo!"

I stopped suddenly, and he stopped too. "Only chickens?" I asked him. "No ducks?"

Jake shook his head. "Nah, Agnes only raised chickens, at least that I ever saw."

That's when I figured out that we put the swimming chickens in the right coop after all.

The wind changed, and I could hear the peeping from the chicks, loud and clear.

Jake grinned. "Can I meet your chicks?"

Everyone looked at me.

I wanted to say no, Agnes. Some people in town know I have your unusual chickens, but knowing that and seeing a chick breathing fire are probably two different things. You always told me to keep them safe, and I try really hard to do that.

But when Jake was younger, you invited him to see your farm. He'd heard and probably seen your chickens before. He cared about Redwood Farm too, I could tell.

So I nodded. I didn't tell him that they were unusual, or warn him to be careful. I led him to the duck coop, which I guess is really a coop for swimming chickens, and stood back and let him see the dark brownish-gray chicks paddling around the pond in a way that Chris said would be impossible for any other chickens, while the light gray chick stood on dry land and watched.

Then the light gray chick turned its head to look at me, peeped a few times, and shot a little tiny jet of flame out of its beak. It blinked, rubbed its beak on its fluffy shoulder, fell over, and went to sleep.

Jake grinned. "They're so cute!" he said happily. "Seriously, I never get over how cute chicks are. And the noises they make!"

"Yeah," I said. Maybe Jake hadn't noticed what the chicks were doing. Maybe he wore glasses and forgot them in the car.

"Do you like having chickens? What do you like best? Do you think you'll ever hatch chicks again?" Jake asked.

"I love having chickens!" I told him. "I never had any pets at all before, but I know chickens are the best—except maybe Sam's llama, who is very cool too, of course. I love how they bulldoze all the weeds and all the dirt goes flying, and how they always look really serious, even when they're molting and funny-looking, and all the sounds they make, and how they will jump for a tomato but look kind of mad about it, and how they're pretty much the only kind of pet except ducks and geese and maybe quail or emus that will lay eggs you can eat for breakfast."

"And ostriches," Chris reminded me. "And maybe turkeys."

I nodded. "Yeah, I guess." I tried to remember what Jake's third question was. "I'll probably need to hatch chicks again. Redwood Farm is my responsibility, after all. I was pretty nervous about it, and sometimes it was hard to know what to do, or what not to do, but Chris and Sam and Xochi and Lupe and this lady named Hort helped me a lot. I bet it will be easier next time." I shrugged. "I'm glad you think the farm looks better now, but it's still awfully empty, don't you think? I'd like to fill all Redwood Farm's coops with chickens again, so I'll hatch as many chicks as I need to." If the inspector lets me, I thought, and I looked across the field to the front hedge. But no one was in sight.

Jake nodded. "Isn't it hard, though? Being in school

and having homework and having to take care of a whole farm too?"

I shrugged. "You did it," I reminded him. "Maybe not a whole farm, but your chickens. I was really glad to have help getting things ready here."

"Sophie works hard," Xochi told him seriously. "But her friends help too."

"We like helping Sophie out," Sam told him. "I mean, I have to take care of my llama, Ella, and I have other chores, but that doesn't mean I can't come help mow the grass sometimes, and pick apples."

Chris nodded. "It goes pretty fast with Gregory's riding mower," he said. "And people liked Agnes, and they want to help Soph with Redwood Farm. Besides, it's fun to pick apples and eat pizza. Not that your dad has to give us pizza every time."

"I guess I do it differently than Agnes did," I told Jake. "Gregory said Agnes didn't even want him to help her. But it doesn't seem . . ." I hesitated, and then I told him what I really thought. "It doesn't seem fair to the chickens to turn down help, if it makes their lives better and safer."

I'm sorry if that's a hard truth, Agnes. I know you always tried to do your best too. But that's how it looks to me right now.

Jake looked thoughtful for a minute, and then he nodded. "I can see that," he said.

Sam was checking her watch and starting to get anxious, I noticed. "Could you just see if there's anyone out front?" I asked her. "Sorry, Jake—someone else is supposed to come soon, and I don't want to miss them."

Sam nodded and took off, and Chris and Xochi went with her.

"You have really good friends," Jake said.

I nodded. "Chris is a poultry farmer too—he made sure I didn't help the chicks when they were hatching. Xochi is learning to be a zookeeper, so she knows all kinds of things about animals. And Sam's going to learn about chickens now too. We built a coop for the place where her granddad lives, so everyone can watch chickens when they feel like it. Chris did the design, and Lupe led the building, and Sam got permission, and Xochi scheduled their care."

"Neat!" Jake said, smiling. "Will some of your chickens live there?"

And, the way he asked it, I knew he had been paying attention after all. He'd seen what the chicks were doing, and he definitely knew about your unusual chickens.

I shook my head. "My chickens aren't a good fit for a retirement home," I told him. "Sam's family bought some regular pullets from Jane's feedstore—Easter Eggers, I think. My chickens are better for experienced poultry farmers. Besides, I'm busy filling up Agnes's coops again; I'm not going to be selling chickens for a long time. Maybe not even until I'm eighteen."

Lupe rolled her eyes. "Ancient, like me!" she said, poking me.

I ignored her. "I want to do it right," I told him. "Maybe things will change, but that's how I see it now."

He nodded. "I did a project on a farm once that was bringing a chicken breed back from near-extinction," he said. "Chickens aren't going extinct, of course, but there weren't very many left of this particular breed. By the time the poultry farmers were ready to sell some, they had a waiting list a mile long. It can work." He smiled at me. "I bet my aunt would want to be on your list."

I nodded. I could give Ms. O'Malley the Redwood Farm Quiz someday, and see if she was ready for unusual chickens.

"Hey, thanks for showing me around, Sophie. I really appreciate it," Jake said.

"No problem. Just let me know if you ever want to come again," I said. Then I looked back at the chicks once more. "I might have more questions for you too. Is it okay if I email you sometime?"

"Of course," Jake said. "Your cousin has my email address." He grinned at Lupe, and she grinned back.

Chris, Xochi, and Sam hadn't come back yet, and I

was starting to get anxious too. Jake saw me looking at the front path, and nodded. "I'd better get going."

"Thanks for coming by," I told him. "Say hi to your aunt for me, and tell your dad again that everyone really liked his pizza, okay?"

He laughed. "Sure. He knows. But I'll tell him anyway. See you around."

Lupe and I watched him walk along the path and out the gate. Then we raced each other across the lawn to see what happened to Sam, Chris, Xochi, and the inspector.

But Chris, Sam, and Xochi were just hanging out in the front parking space, waving as Jake drove off down the road. "We figured we'd better wait here so we could tell the inspector where to park," Sam said. "But no one came by."

Chris shrugged. "Maybe traffic is bad."

So we waited in front of Redwood Farm for a whole hour. Lupe and Xochi sang a Bomba Estéreo song that Sam and Chris wanted to learn, and I did some of the moves. But the inspector never came. Lupe said it couldn't be my fault if I was where I was supposed to be, when I was supposed to be there, and we'd just have to reschedule. So, finally, we went home and made apple crisp.

It was delicious.

Your friend,
Soph

PS I tried calling that number, but all I got was a recording that said the office was closed on weekends. I guess I'll try again next week.

Dear Sophie—

I thought you might want a copy of the report I filed. You'll be receiving an official letter soon. Let me know if you have any questions.

Sincerely,

Jake

PS Sorry I didn't tell you why I was really there. My job is to gather data in situations like this, and we get better information when people aren't trying to impress us. But everything I told you was true.

OFFICIAL REPORT FOR REDWOOD FARM

Owner: Sophie Brown
Stock: Unusual chickens (various breeds and abilities)
Inspected by: Jacob Lee, Junior Inspector for Northern California, Sonoma County office
Date of inspection: Saturday, September 27
Reporting on: The hatching of a fire-breathing chicken from a clutch of Mille Fleur d'Uccle Swimmers, and whether this new breed should remain at Redwood Farm or be transferred to secure facilities elsewhere for care and research.

SCORECARD:

(On a scale of 1 to 10, with 1 being the least likely, and 10 being the most likely)

1. How likely is the poultry farmer to request help when necessary? 10
2. How likely is the poultry farmer to provide a safe, secure environment for poultry? 8
3. How likely is the poultry farmer to refuse to sell poultry to someone who is not prepared for unusual poultry, or cannot properly care for unusual poultry? 9
4. How likely is the poultry farmer to refuse to sell poultry to someone who might cause trouble for unusual poultry? 9

5. How likely is the new chicken breed to thrive in this farm's environment and with this farmer's care? 8

6. What is the poultry farmer's experience level?
   Beginner = 0
   Intermediate = 1
   Experienced = 2
   1
   _____

7. What level does the situation require?
   Beginner = 0
   Intermediate = 1
   Experienced = 2
   2
   _____

HOW TO CALCULATE THE SCORE:

Add up the points given for questions 1 through 6. Subtract any points given for question 7 from the total. Score: 43 out of 52 possible points

COMMENTS:

Sophie Brown is a responsible poultry farmer who does not allow her lack of experience to prevent her from providing excellent care for her chickens. Upon inheriting an unusual poultry farm in disrepair, she used creative problem-solving to bring her friends and family in to help fix the farm up again, creating new ties between the farm and the community. She has worked hard to learn what she needs to know, and is not afraid to ask questions. Upon learning of the upcoming inspection, Sophie increased her efforts to do what's right for the chickens in her care, including requesting assistance from someone she has not always gotten along with. Finally, Sophie helped build a chicken coop for mundane chickens at a local retirement home, strengthening her ties to the community and increasing goodwill toward chickens, while sensibly deciding that such a public space was not a good fit for unusual chickens.

"Sophie Brown reads every book on chickens I find for her. She's constantly adding to her poultry knowledge."—Grace O'Malley, town librarian and vice president of the local American Poultry Association chapter

"Sophie never hesitates to tackle a responsibility, no matter how big it is, and always works hard and does her best. I'm proud to know her."—Gregory Buchanan, postal worker and 4-H leader

"Sophie Brown never turns down an offer of help for her chickens. I admire that."—Susan Griegson, president of the local American Poultry Association chapter

"I am writing to inform the Committee of this new breed, as required. But if you take that chick away from Sophie Brown, you will lose the trust and respect of one of the most promising unusual poultry farmers I've met, and mine too."—Hortensia James, unusual poultry farmer, A Peculiar Kind of Bird Poultry Farm

WHAT RECOMMENDATIONS DOES THE INSPECTOR MAKE FOR THIS SITUATION?

The new fire-breathing chick (possibly a Porcelain d'Uccle) is undoubtedly an expert-level chick. Sophie Brown has become an intermediate-level poultry farmer in only a few months, but will require significantly more expertise to successfully raise a breed with such a challenging ability.

However, Sophie Brown has shown great ingenuity and responsibility, working closely with the local fire department to take precautionary measures, which have passed their inspection. The chick is thriving with its flock mates, and seems unlikely to injure them, due to their unusual abilities.

It is the recommendation of this inspector that such a promising poultry farmer not be discouraged by the removal of this new breed, but rather supported in her ongoing learning. In addition, the inspector notes the difficulty of finding more suitable flock mates for a chick with this ability, and the danger of loneliness among flock animals kept by themselves. Therefore, this inspector recommends that the new chick remain in Sophie Brown's care at Redwood Farm, and that this inspector become her mentor, providing the expert-level assistance this breed may require.

Regular reports will, of course, be filed.

Bantam Mille Fleur Swimmer
Belgian Bearded d'Uccle

Diminutive height, reddish-brown plumage with
black bars and white spangles, and black tail.
Full beard, feathered legs and feet. Red serrated
single comb. *Possibly webbed toes.*

    Small creamy white eggs, good production.
Good with people; a favorite with many unusual
chicken farmers. *Can swim.*

Unusual Poultry Committee, Northern California Division

Tuesday, September 30

Ms. Sophie Brown
Redwood Farm
Gravenstein, CA 95472

Dear Ms. Sophie Brown,

As recommended following your inspection, the Unusual Poultry Committee has decided to leave the sole individual of the new breed of poultry in your care, provided you accept the following conditions:

1. You will become the apprentice of Inspector Jacob Lee, who will provide guidance as needed.
2. You will contact Mr. Lee or another experienced unusual poultry farmer at once if you experience any emergency situation.
3. You are able to assure the Committee that Redwood Farm will not remain unoccupied.

Do you agree to accept responsibility for raising this new breed, with the above conditions?

__X__ Yes, I accept responsibility, and agree to the above conditions.

____No, please remove this new breed from my care.

Please return one signed copy to the Unusual Poultry Committee for our records, keeping one copy for your own records.

Signed: <u>Sophia Mariposa Brown</u>

Date: Thursday, October 2
To: Hortensia James <hjames@APeculiarKindofBird.com>
From: Sophie Brown <unusualchickenfarmer@gmail.com>
Subject: Thank you

Dear Hort,

I know you had to do what you thought was right. But I appreciate you speaking your truths to the inspector too, and sticking up for me and my chick. I guess you did your own observations instead of making assumptions about a kid who didn't have a certificate or anything.

    Thank you for believing in me.

Your friend,
Soph

PS Maybe you already heard that I'm going to be a real apprentice now. I might have questions for you too, so can I keep emailing you?

PPS Here's a picture of my chicks in their new coop at Redwood Farm. Sorry it's a little blurry. They move fast.

Date: Thursday, October 2
To: Sophie Brown <unusualchickenfarmer@gmail.com>
From: Hortensia James <hjames@APeculiarKindofBird.com>
Subject: RE: Thank you

Dear Sophie,

You can always email me. I'd like to stay in touch, even when you don't have questions.

Your friend,

Hort

Blackbird Farm

Saturday, October 4

Mariposa García González

Heaven

Querida Abuelita,

Today we had the best apple-picking party ever. I wish you could have been there too. You would have loved it.

Xochi and her family came, and Jake and Ms. O'Malley, and Chris and his mom, and Sam and her parents, and Gregory and his friend George, and Al, and Jane and Violet, and Joy, and you know what? I invited Ms. Griegson, and she came too. After all, there were a LOT of apples to pick.

After we picked every single apple from every single tree, we had a picnic. We had seven kinds of crisp!! Apple crisp that Chris and his mom made, blackberry crisp that Sam and her dad made, plum crisp that Dad made all by himself, apple-blackberry crisp that Lupe and Mom made (they wanted to try making some too), and plum-apple crisp, blackberry-plum crisp, and apple-blackberry-plum crisp that Dad and I made. (Apple-blackberry-plum was my favorite!) We also had a tomato salad from Joy's garden, zucchini spread from Jane and Violet's garden, breadsticks from Jake's dad, Ms. O'Malley's special applesauce, long skinny cookies called Pocky that Al brought, pickled carrots that Ms. Griegson brought, Gregory's favorite potato salad, and esquites from Xochi's family. (As soon as Gregory took one bite of that corn, he said he had to have the recipe, so Dad translated for him and Xochi's abuela.)

We had to make two trips, even with our car and Lupe's, because you can't tip a crisp on its side or stack it on top of another crisp, and we had all of Lupe's stuff too, because she moved to Redwood Farm today. I'm going to miss her a lot, but I'll still see her every day, and I'm glad she'll be there for the chicks. I know she can handle it. I don't know if Mom and Dad will ever really believe that she didn't do anything wrong, but after she signed up with my school for all her volunteer hours, and got written up in the paper for becoming our club leader, and got an A on her college paper about our building-stuff club, and after Tía Gabriela called Mom and Tía Catalina and threatened to tell me and Lupe and Javier about all the mistakes they made when they were teenagers, Mom and Dad and Tía Catalina and Tío Fernando decided Lupe could try living at Redwood Farm. I taught her how to give the chicks food and water without letting them out of the coop, just in case, but I'll still check on them every day.

We had all kinds of things to celebrate—more good things than I ever could imagine!

Ella won a red ribbon in the llama show (and didn't spit on anyone this time).

Chris gets to go spend the weekend with his dad and see a soccer game in the city.

Chris's mom gets a quiet weekend in her garden.

We're crossing our fingers for Jake, who is trying to buy a piece of land from another farmer, so he can maybe start his own poultry farm.

Gregory got a promotion—he's the head of our post office now! But he says he'll still bring our mail.

Ms. O'Malley got a grant for twenty new books at the library. She says at least one will definitely be about chickens.

Joy got an award for one of her photographs. They're going to print it in the big-city paper so everyone can see teenagers reading at the library.

Al learned how to do the Funky Chicken and the Macarena, and she tried to teach us how to moonwalk. I need more practice.

The feedstore is doing well, and so is Jane and Violet's farm—maybe even so well that Violet can look for a job closer to home soon.

Ms. Griegson is getting a special new kind of chick (but not an unusual kind): Swedish Flower hens. She seems excited.

Lupe got her A, and gets to try living on her own.

Dad sold our grapes and made some money.

Mom got the lead article in a major magazine, and you know what? It's about the chicken coop we built for Sam's granddad!

And Xochi's parents decided she can have chickens! You know what else was neat? Chris and Sam were almost as excited for her as I was. We're going to help her build her coop next.

As for me, I'm going to be an unusual poultry apprentice, and learn how to take care of enough unusual chickens to fill every coop at Redwood Farm.

Maybe everything does work out sometimes, when you try your best.

Te quiero,
Soficita

Porcelain
Bantam ~~Mille Fleur~~
Belgian Bearded d'Uccle
Sparkie

    Diminutive height, ~~reddish-brown~~ *(beige)* plumage with *(blue)* ~~black~~ bars and white spangles, and ~~black~~ *(blue)* tail. Full beard, feathered legs and feet. Red serrated single comb.

    Small creamy white eggs, good production. *(Probably???)* ~~Good with people; a favorite with many unusual chicken farmers.~~ For expert unusual chicken farmers only! Can breathe small flames.

Date: Monday, October 6
To: Sophie Brown <unusualchickenfarmer@gmail.com>
From: Betty Johnson <BJohnson@FluffyChickenHatchery.com>
Subject: Egg update

Dear Sophie,

My chickens have finished hatching the zoo's ibises and are beginning to lay again. I'll collect eggs to send to you later this month.

Here's what you'll need:

1 ostrich- or emu-size egg incubator
1 extra-large heat lamp
1 extra-large chick brooder
Poultry feeder
Poultry waterer
<u>Large</u> quantity of chick food
<u>Large</u> quantity of chicken grit
A chicken coop separate from your other chickens

I'll let you know when they're in the mail.

Sincerely,
Betty

Acknowledgments

I can't imagine writing this book without:

My family, with feathers and without, whose support, encouragement, excited squawking, and occasional reality checks have taken me farther than any of us could have imagined.

The writers and readers and friends who keep me going, especially Caroline Stevermer, Brenna Shanks, Mike Denton, Marin Younker, Edith Hope Bishop, Jen Adam, Kim Baker, Melissa Koosman, Liz Wong, Aarene Storms, Alene Moroni, Alison Weatherby, Lish McBride, Dana Sullivan, Courtney Gould, and the wild and wonderful writers and illustrators of SCBWI Western Washington.

The awesome team at Penguin Random House who made it all happen, especially Jenny Brown, Marisa DiNovis, Trish Parcell, Isabel Warren-Lynch, Josh Redlich, Artie Bennett, Lisa Leventer, Deanna Meyerhoff, Adrienne Waintraub, Lisa Nadel, and Kristin Schulz.

Taryn Fagerness, who introduced Sophie to the rest of the world.

Claudia Guadalupe Martínez, Kim Baker, Miriam Rosario, and Jen Adam, who took time from their own amazing books and work to patiently help me get things right.

Molly Baker, who helped Sophie sign her certificates.

Katie Kath, who drew Sophie's world, and who let us see the funniest parts of her life, and the hardest, too.

Mandy Hubbard, who answered every single question I've had on this strange and wonderful journey, and who believed in Sophie before anyone else knew her story.

Nancy Siscoe, who always listened to Sophie, who kept the heart of this book safe every time I lost my way, and whose answer to every question was "More chickens!"

And all the students, teachers, librarians, booksellers, chicken people, and readers who loved Sophie's first adventure, who understand that sometimes funny things and sad things and magic and science are all mixed up together, and who asked what happened next. You're the reason I wrote this book.

PS I hope you like it.